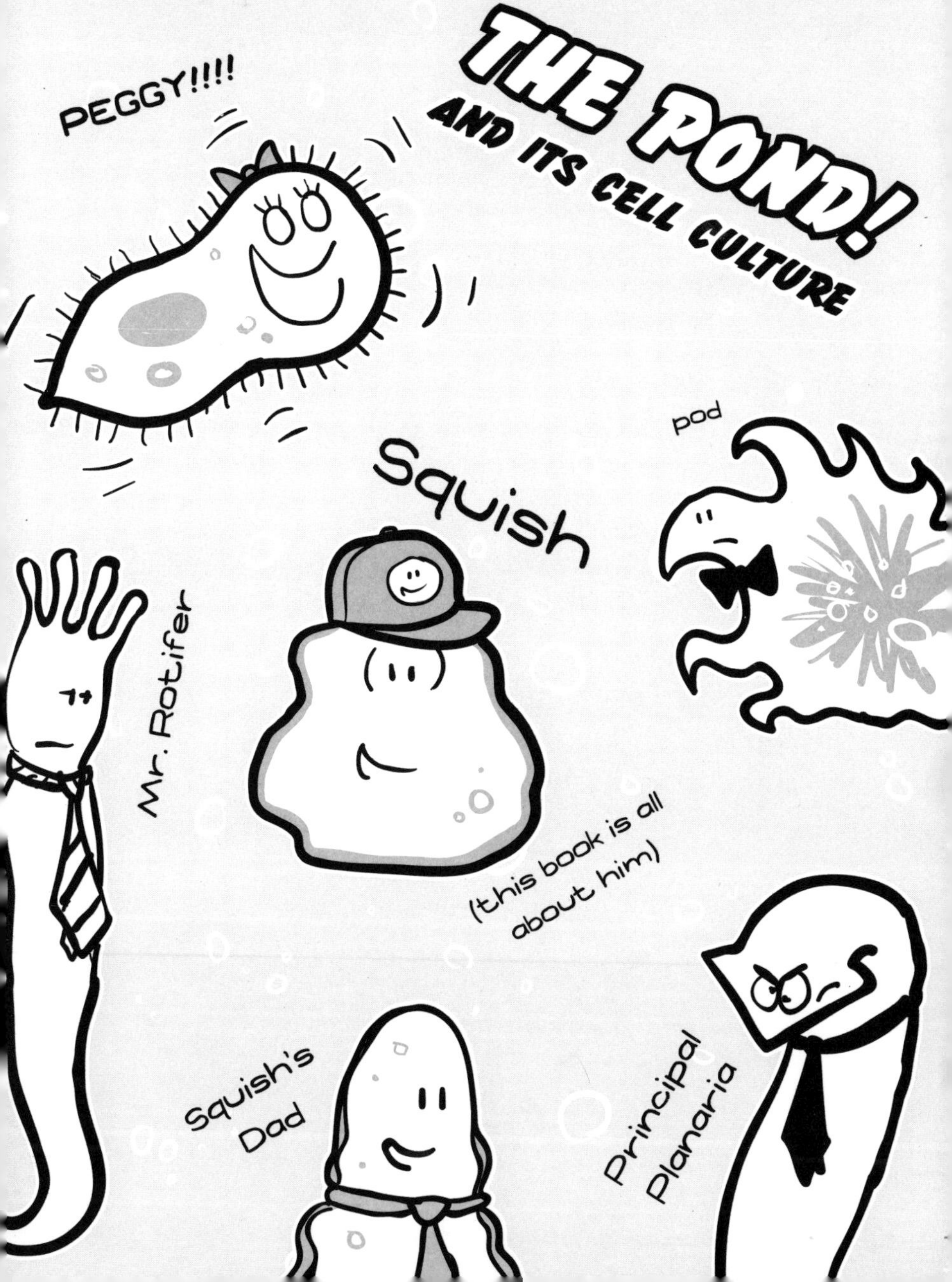
THE POND!
AND ITS CELL CULTURE
PEGGY!!!!
pod
Squish
Mr. Rotifer
(this book is all about him)
Squish's Dad
Principal Planaria

Read ALL the SQUISH books!

#1 SQUISH: Super Amoeba
#2 SQUISH: Brave New Pond
#3 SQUISH: The Power of the Parasite
#4 SQUISH: Captain Disaster
#5 SQUISH: Game On!
#6 SQUISH: Fear the Amoeba
#7 SQUISH: Deadly Disease of Doom

squish
DEADLY DISEASE OF DOOM

BY JENNIFER L. HOLM & MATTHEW HOLM

RANDOM HOUSE 🏠 NEW YORK

Published in the United States by Random House Children's Books,
a division of Penguin Random House LLC, New York.

Random House and the colophon are registered trademarks of
Penguin Random House LLC.

Visit us on the Web! randomhousekids.com

Educators and librarians, for a variety of teaching tools,
visit us at RHTeachersLibrarians.com

Library of Congress Cataloging-in-Publication Data
Holm, Jennifer L.
Deadly disease of doom / by Jennifer L. Holm and Matthew Holm. —
First edition.
p. cm. — (Squish ; #7)
Summary: When Squish, a meek amoeba who loves the comic book
exploits of his favorite hero, "Super Amoeba," starts feeling sick,
he worries he has caught a deadly illness.
ISBN 978-0-307-98305-3 (trade) — ISBN 978-0-307-98306-0 (lib. bdg.) —
ISBN 978-0-307-98307-7 (ebook)
I. Graphic novels. [I. Graphic novels. 2. Amoeba—Fiction. 3. Sick—Fiction.
4. Superheroes—Fiction. 5. Cartoons and comics—Fiction.]
I. Holm, Matthew. II. Title.
PZ7.7.H65De 2015   741.5'973—dc23   2015000928

MANUFACTURED IN MALAYSIA   10 9 8 7 6 5 4 3 2 1
First Edition

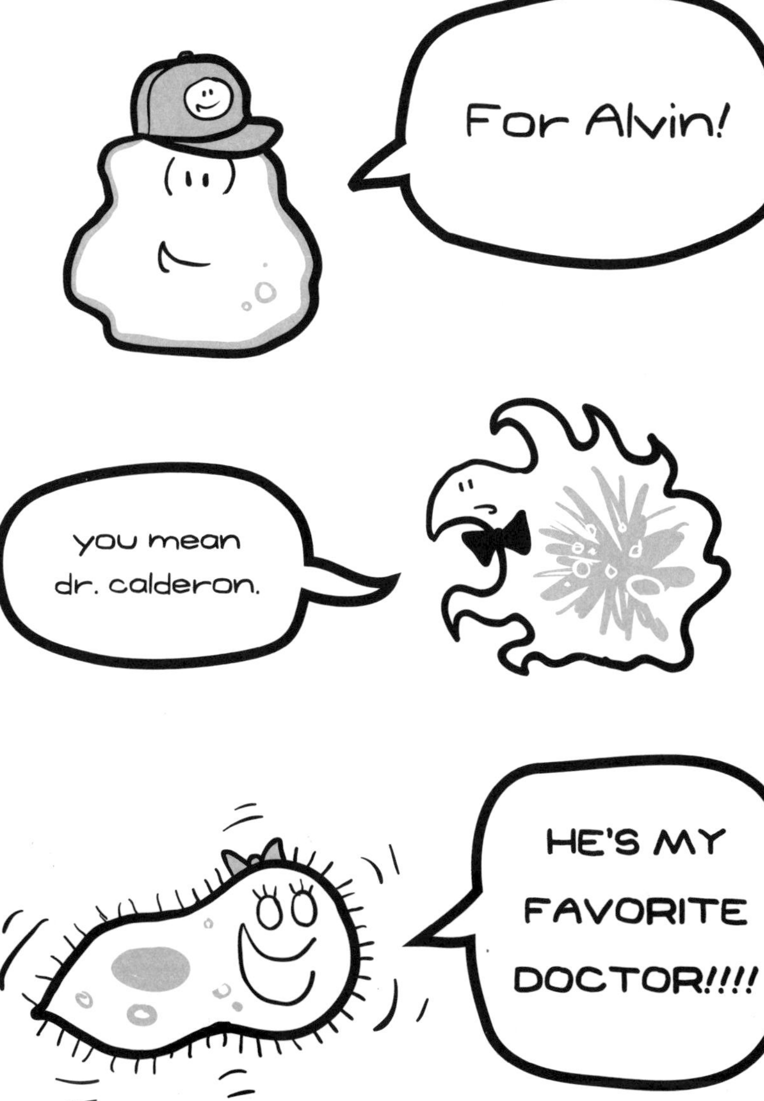
For Alvin!
you mean dr. calderon.
HE'S MY FAVORITE DOCTOR!!!!

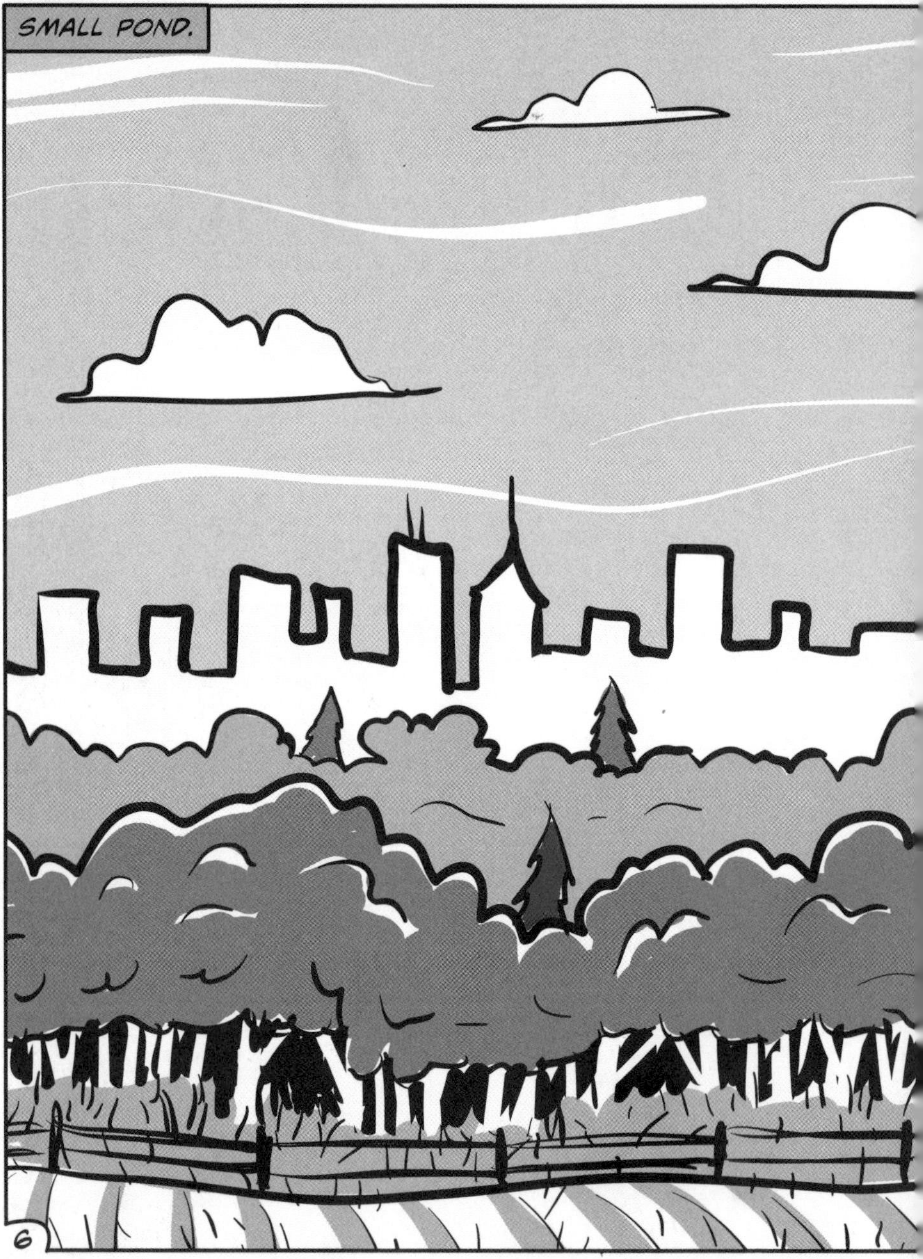
SMALL POND.

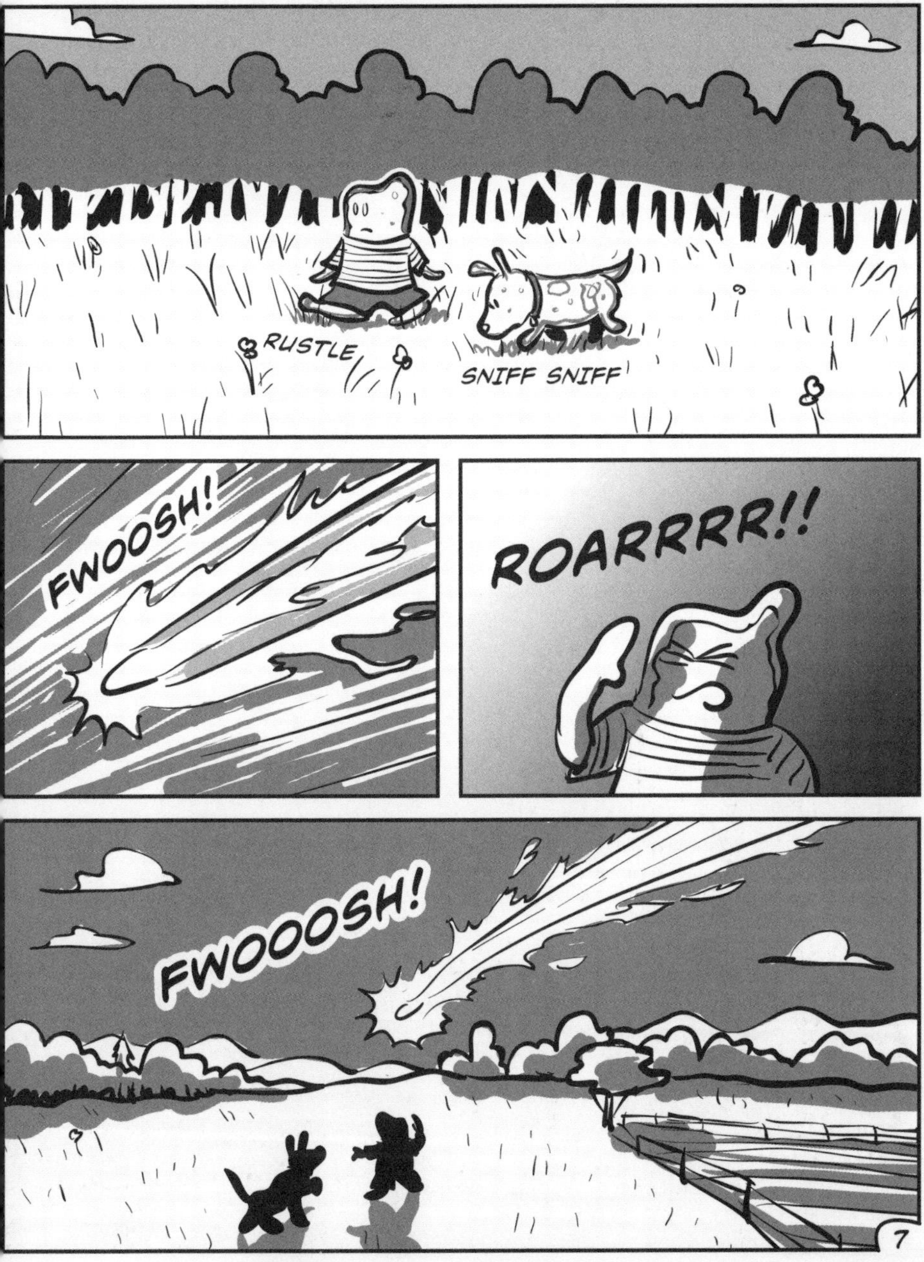
RUSTLE
SNIFF SNIFF
FWOOSH!
ROARRRRR!!
FWOOOOSH!

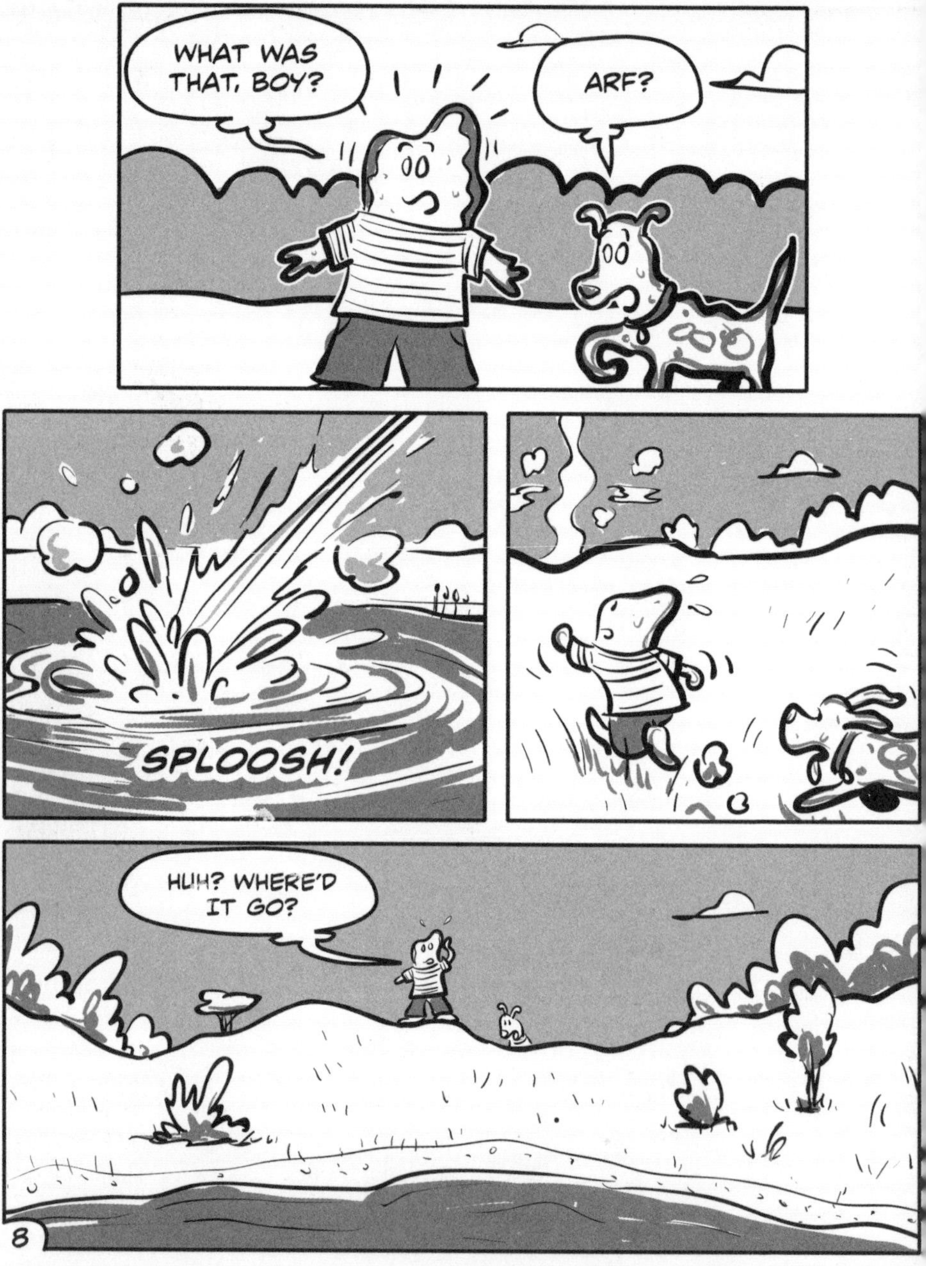
WHAT WAS THAT, BOY?
ARF?
SPLOOSH!
HUH? WHERE'D IT GO?

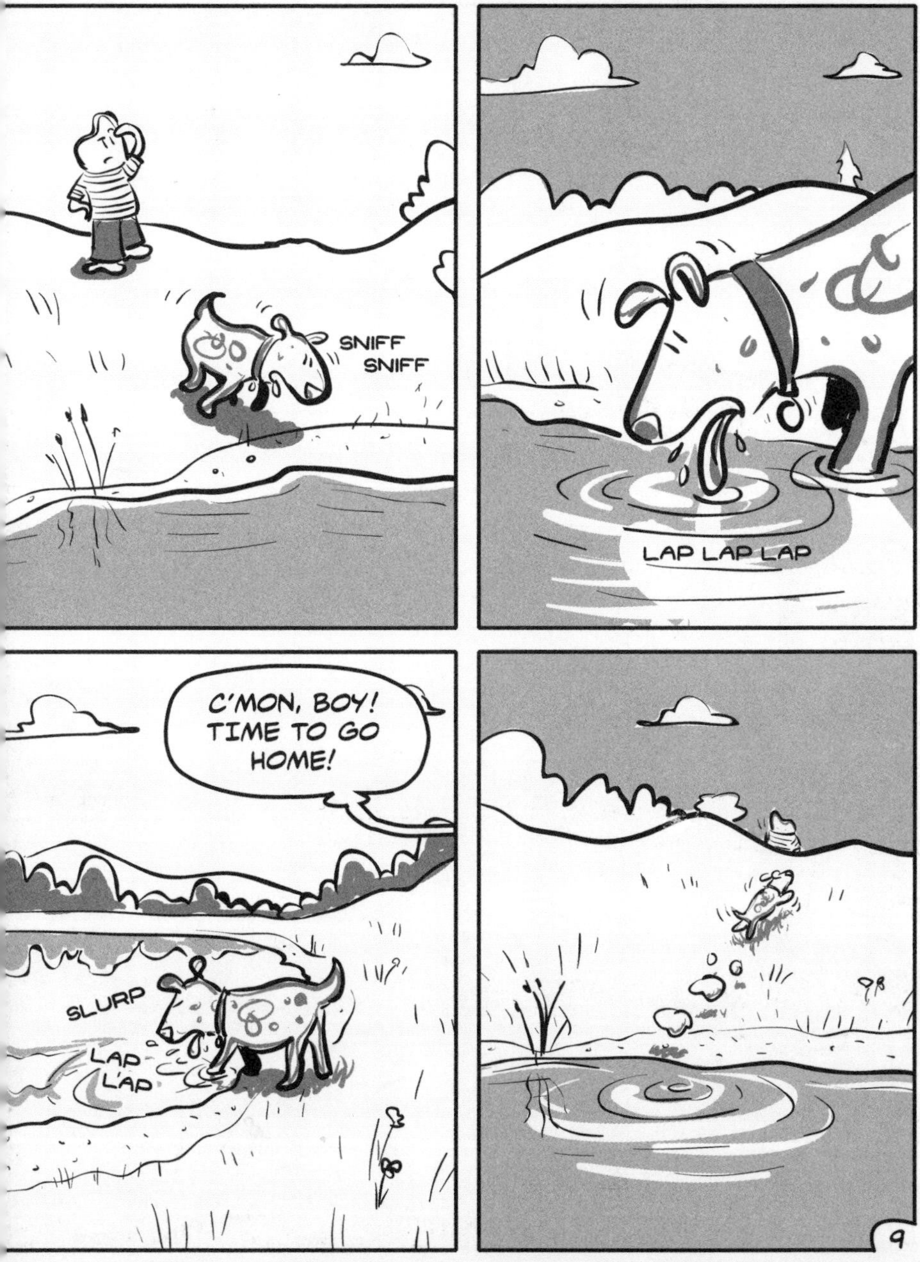
SNIFF
SNIFF
LAP LAP LAP
C'MON, BOY! TIME TO GO HOME!
SLURP
LAP
LAP

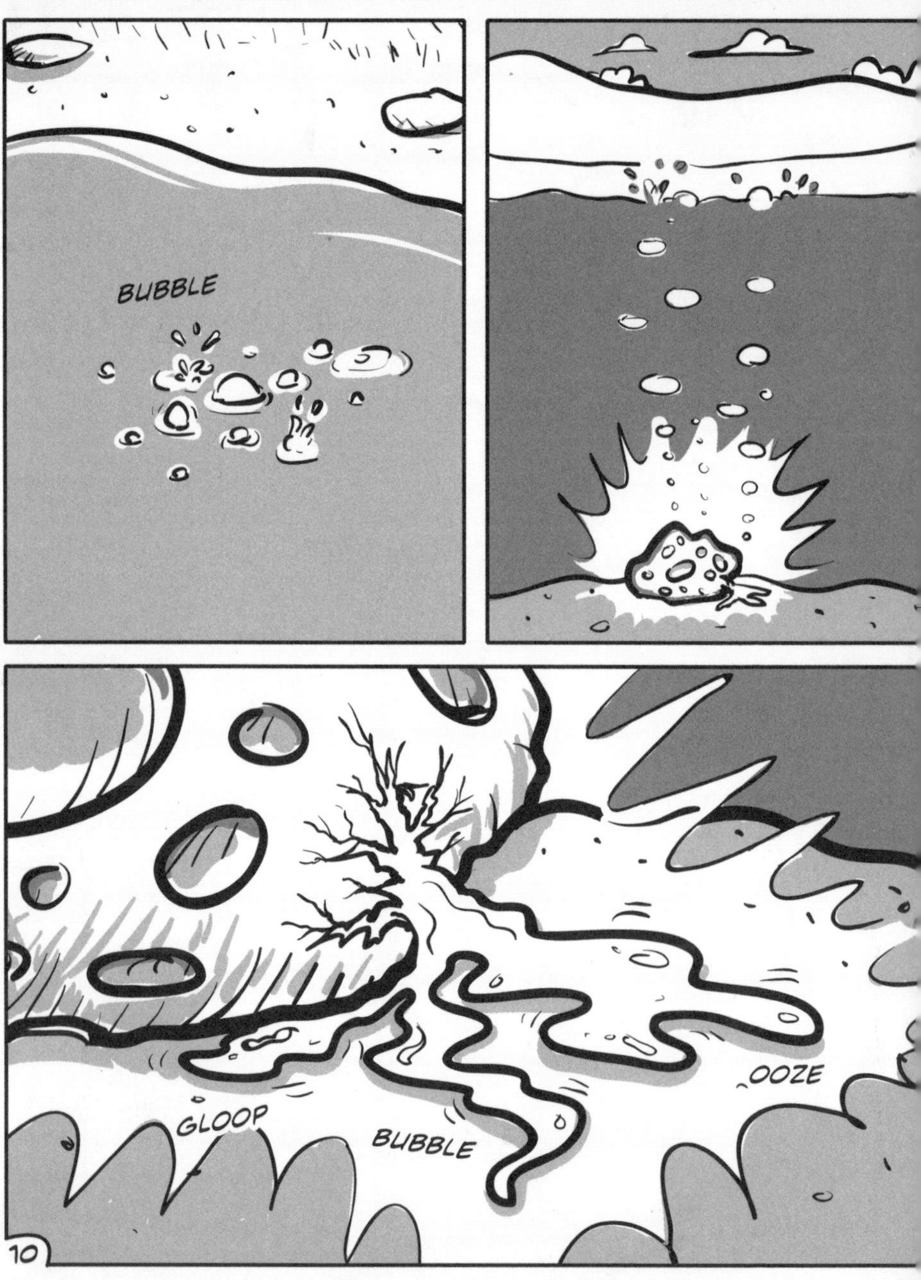
BUBBLE
GLOOP
BUBBLE
OOZE

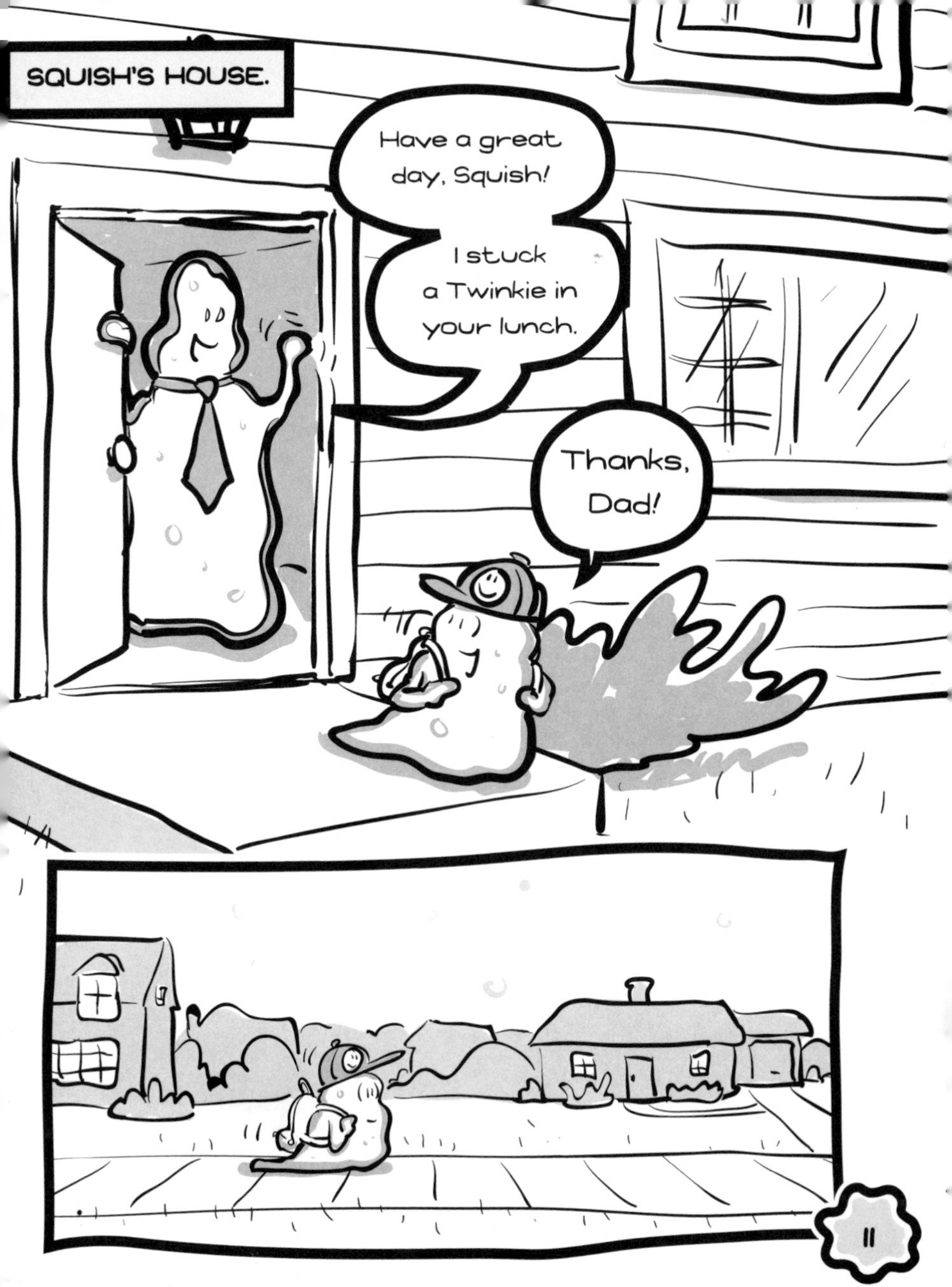
SQUISH'S HOUSE.
Have a great day, Squish!
I stuck a Twinkie in your lunch.
Thanks, Dad!

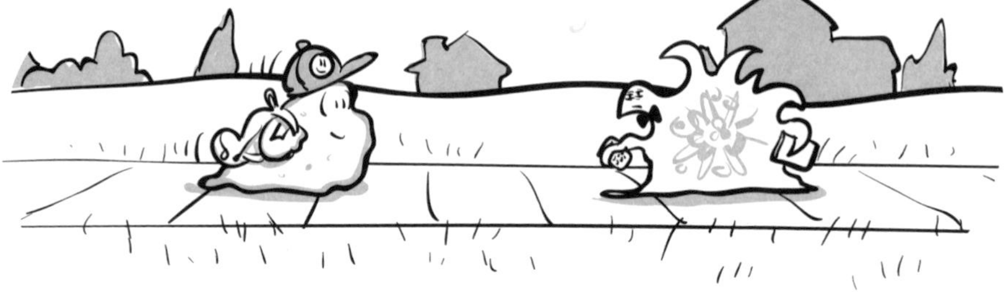

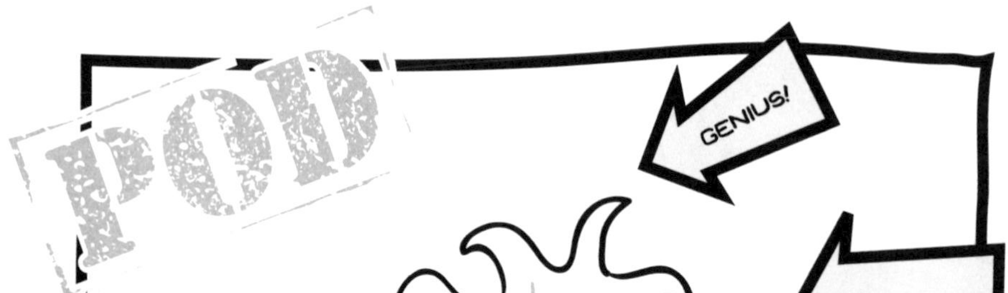
POD
GENIUS!
ALWAYS EATS SQUISH'S TWINKIES!
BEST FRIEND!

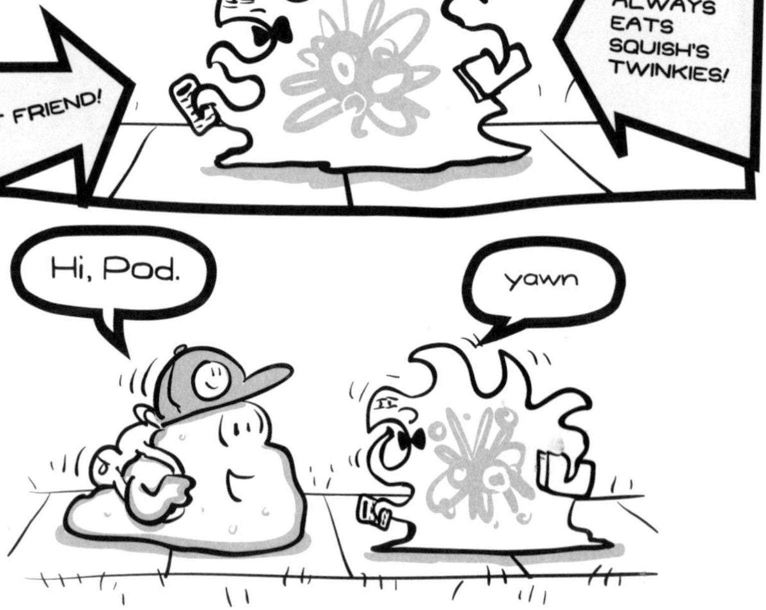
Hi, Pod.
yawn

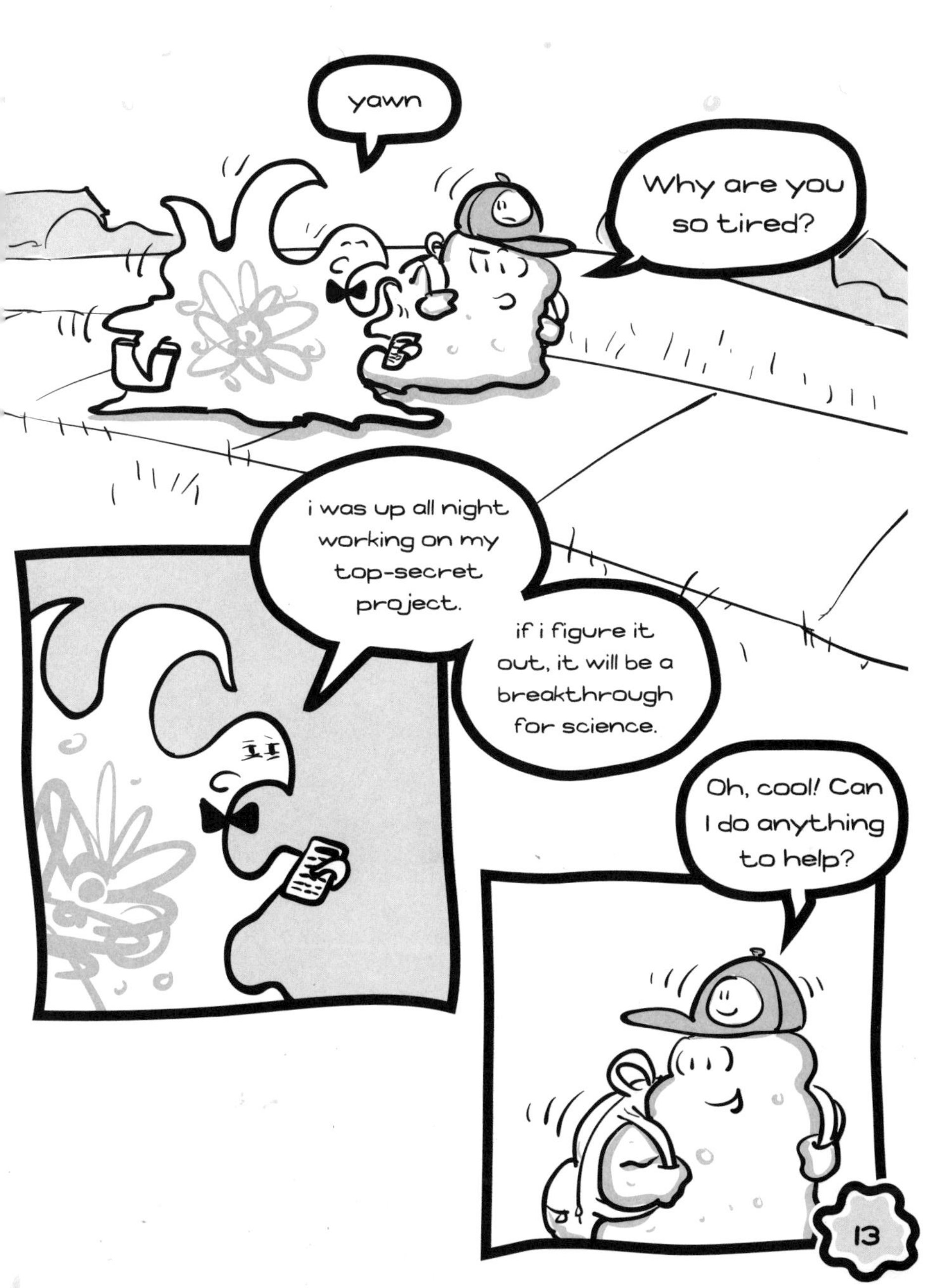
yawn
Why are you so tired?
i was up all night working on my top-secret project.
if i figure it out, it will be a breakthrough for science.
Oh, cool! Can I do anything to help?

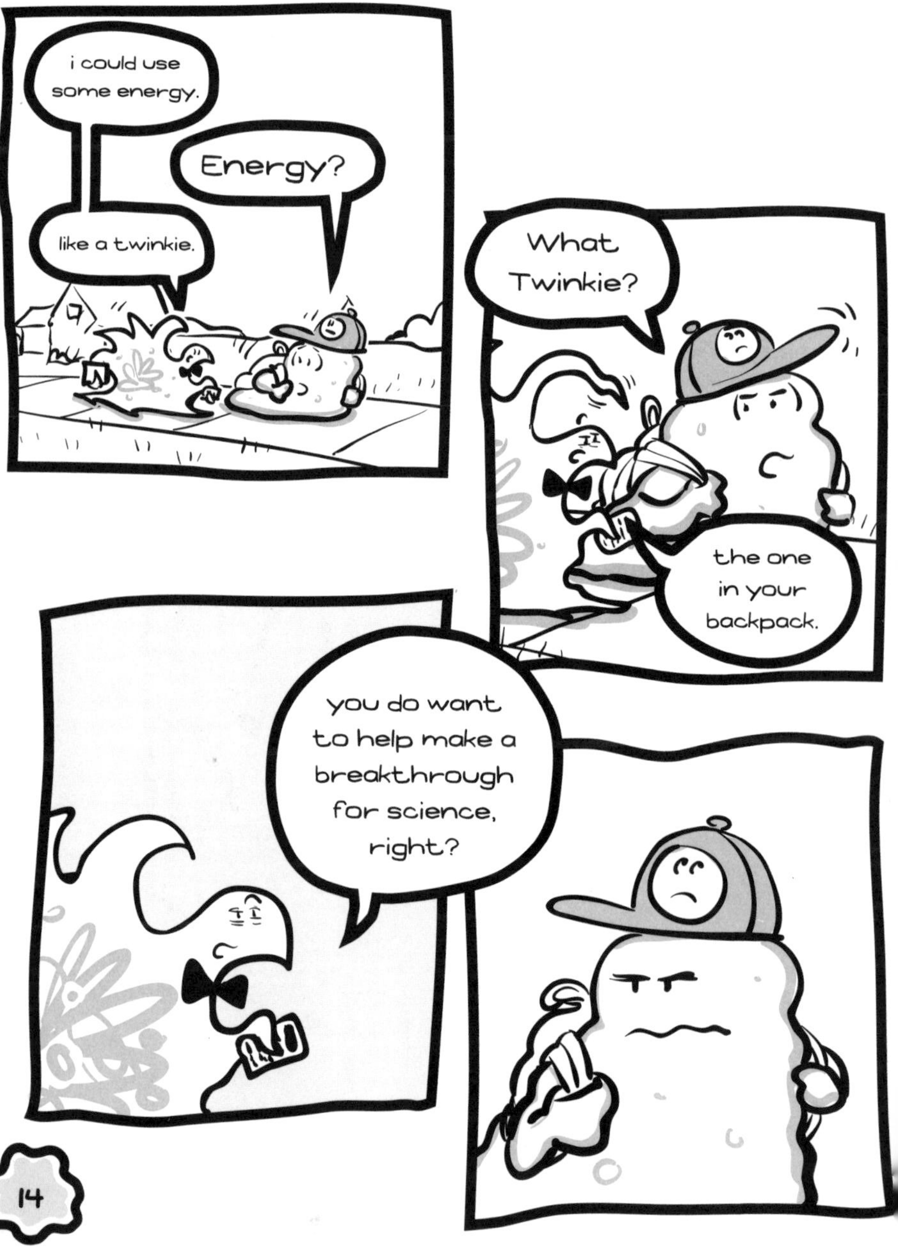
i could use some energy.
Energy?
like a twinkie.
What Twinkie?
the one in your backpack.
you do want to help make a breakthrough for science, right?

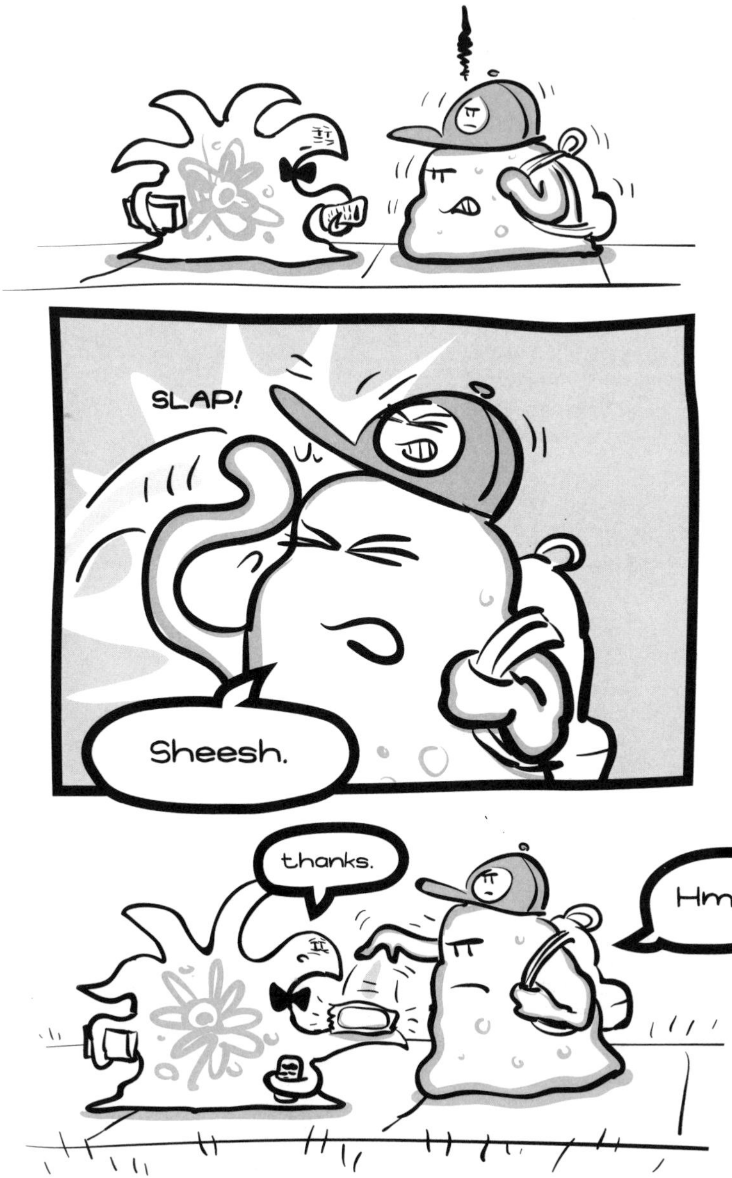
SLAP!
Sheesh.
thanks.
Hmph.

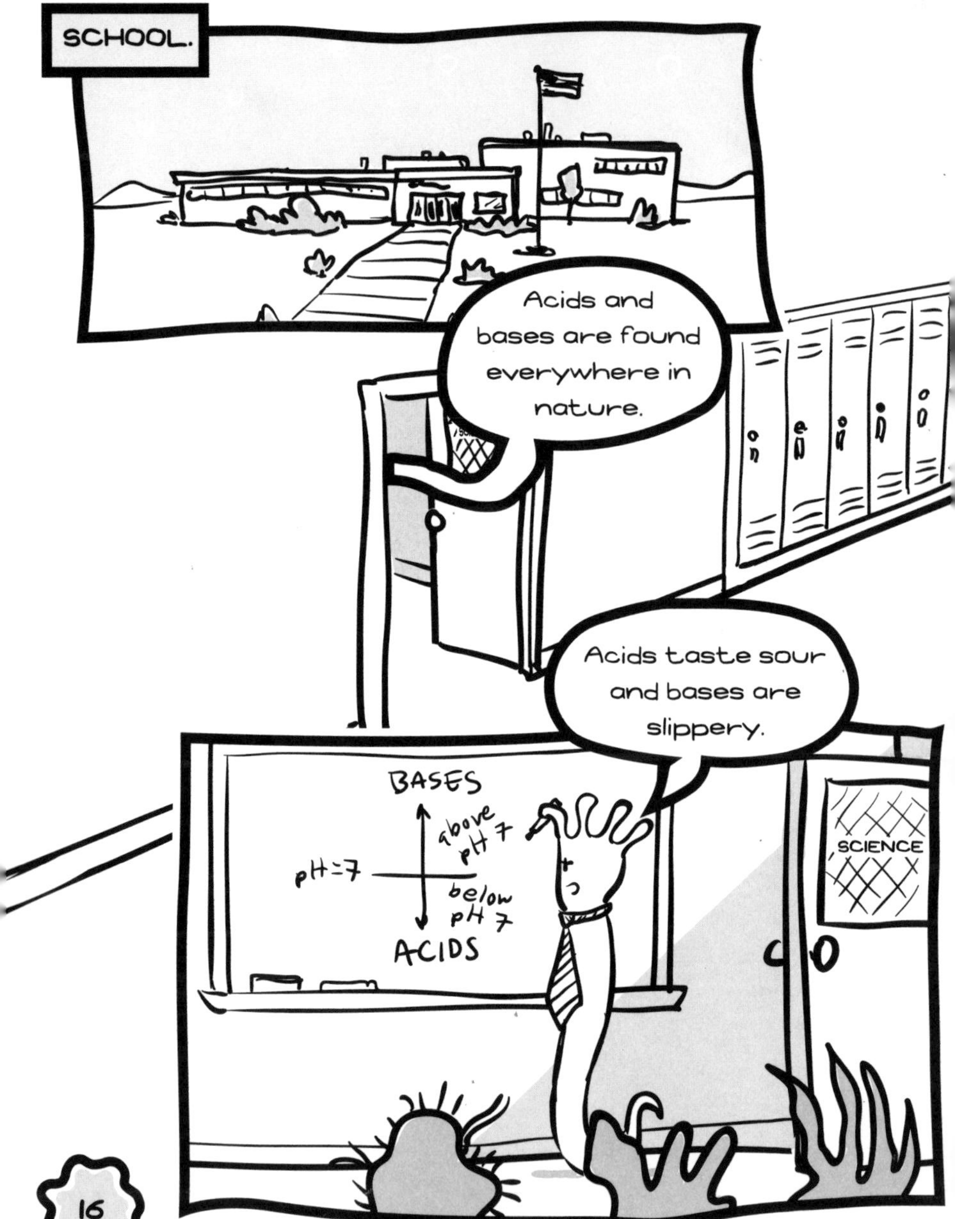
SCHOOL.
Acids and bases are found everywhere in nature.
Acids taste sour and bases are slippery.
BASES
above pH 7
pH=7
below pH 7
ACIDS
SCIENCE

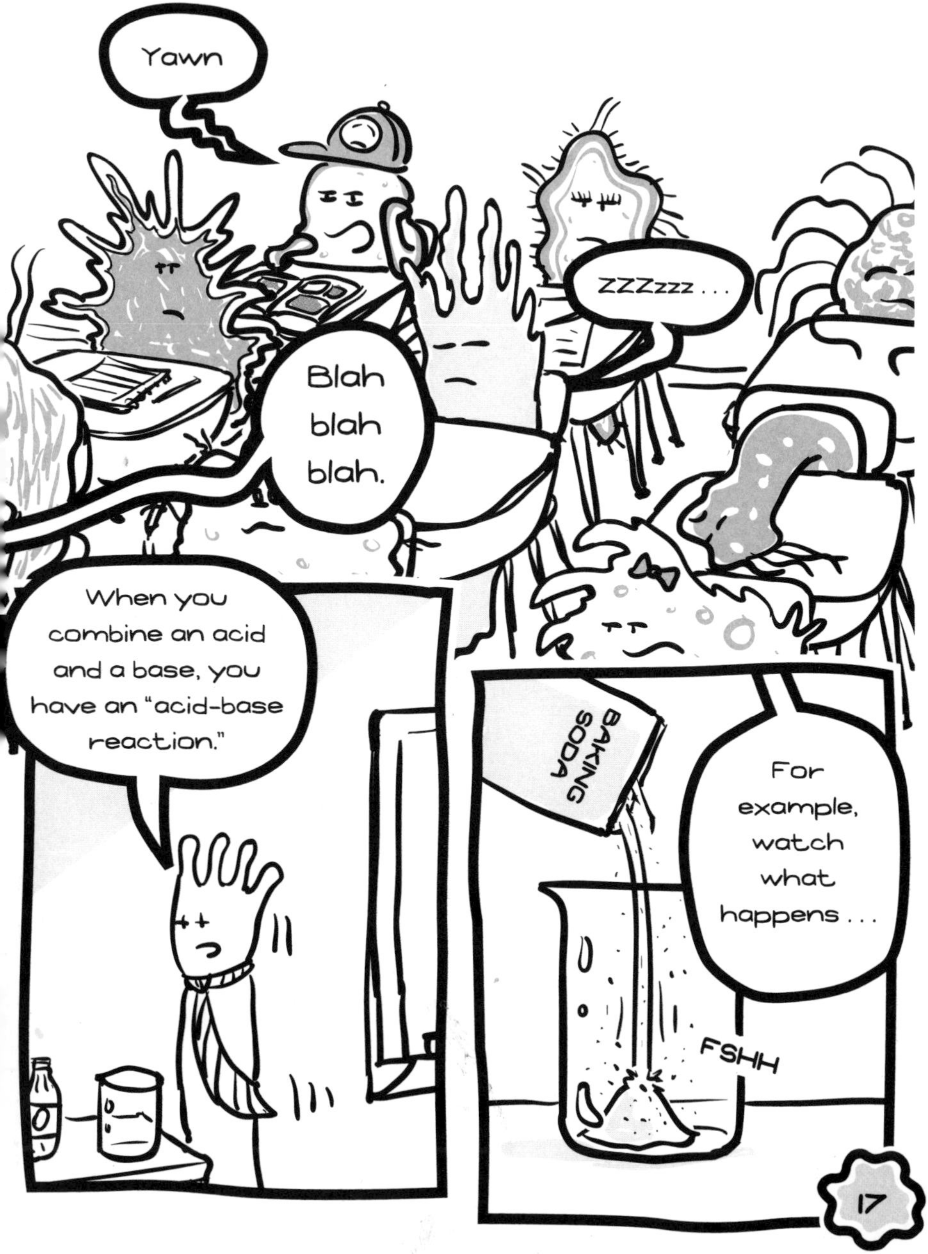

Yawn
ZZZzzz . . .
Blah blah blah.
When you combine an acid and a base, you have an "acid-base reaction."
BAKING SODA
For example, watch what happens . . .
FSHH

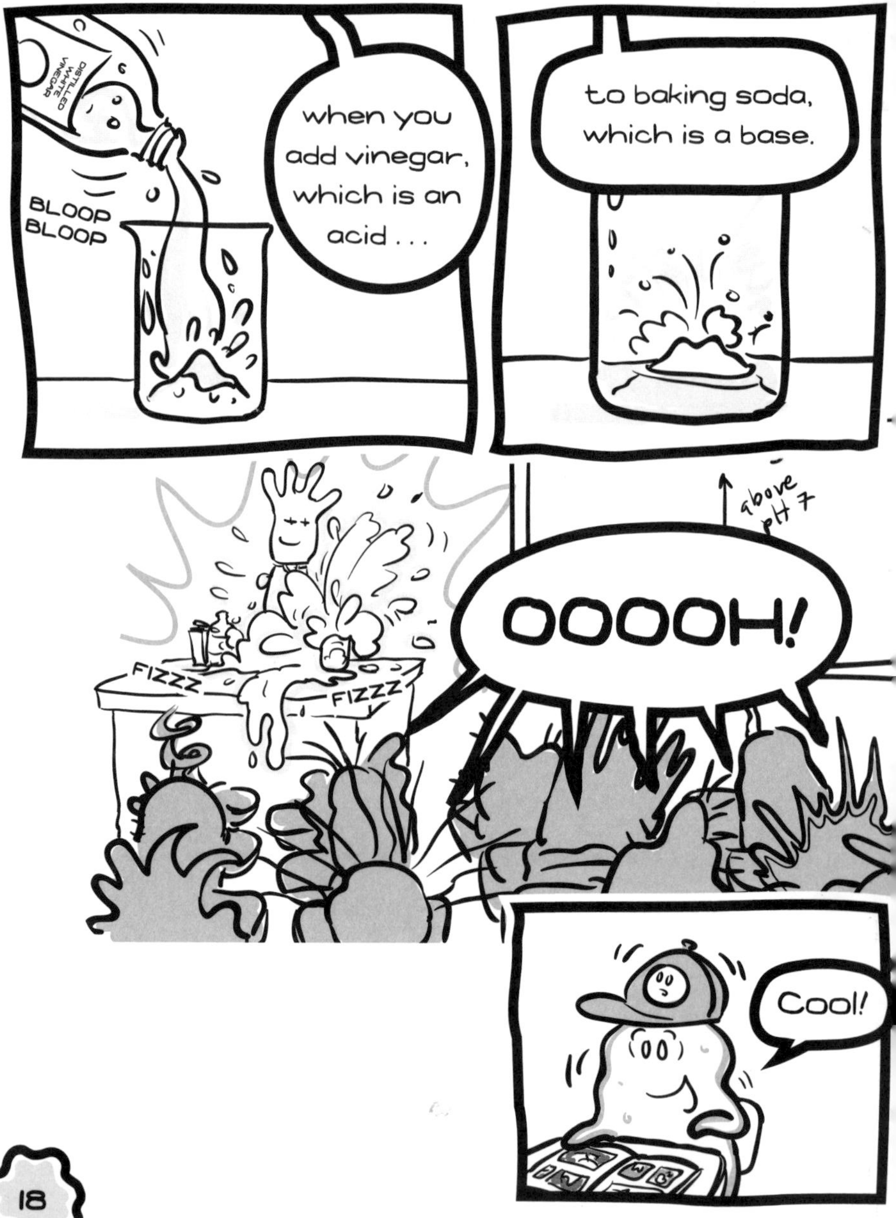
DISTILLED WHITE VINEGAR
BLOOP BLOOP
when you add vinegar, which is an acid . . .
to baking soda, which is a base.
above pH 7
FIZZZ
FIZZZ
OOOOH!
Cool!

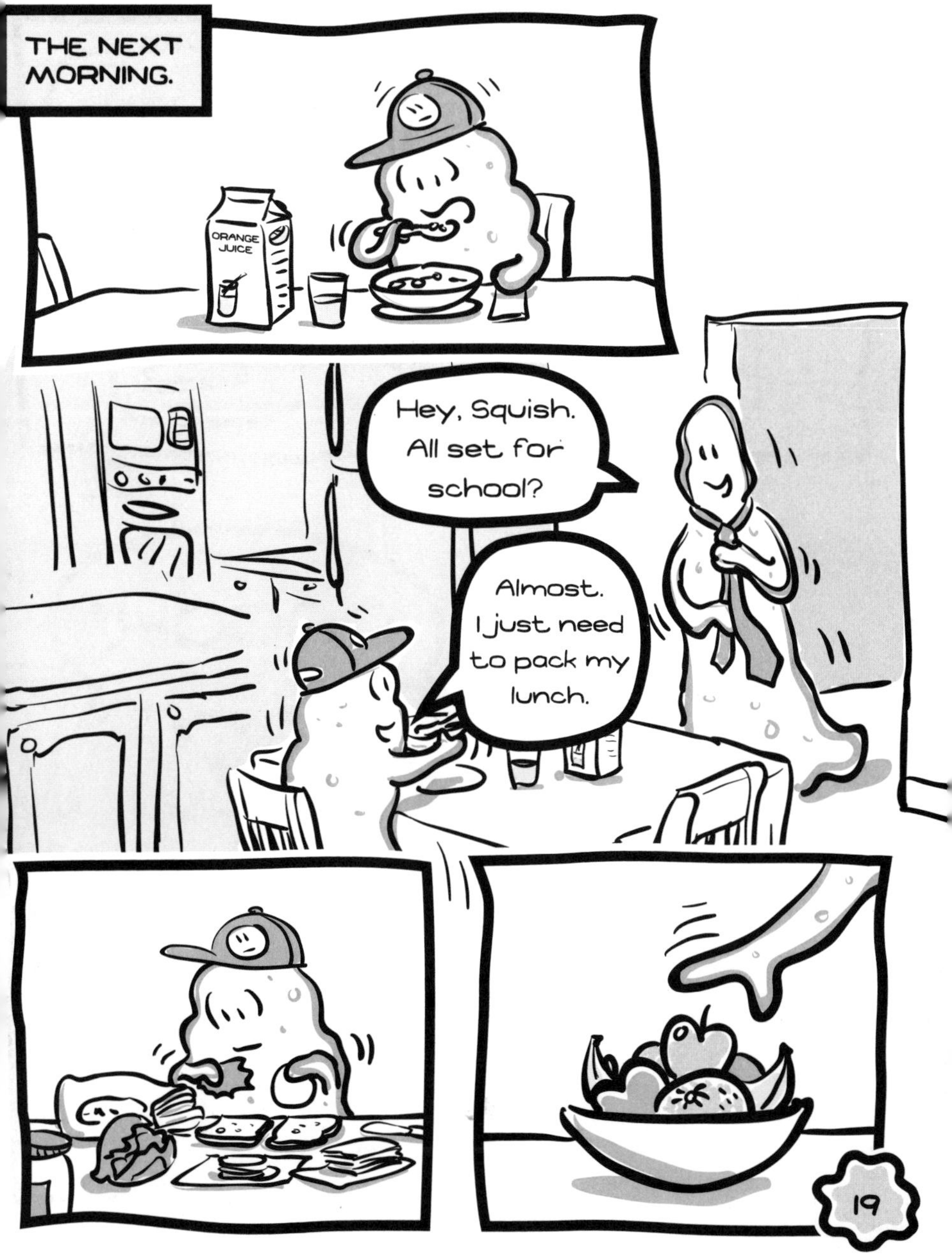
THE NEXT MORNING.
ORANGE JUICE
Hey, Squish. All set for school?
Almost. I just need to pack my lunch.

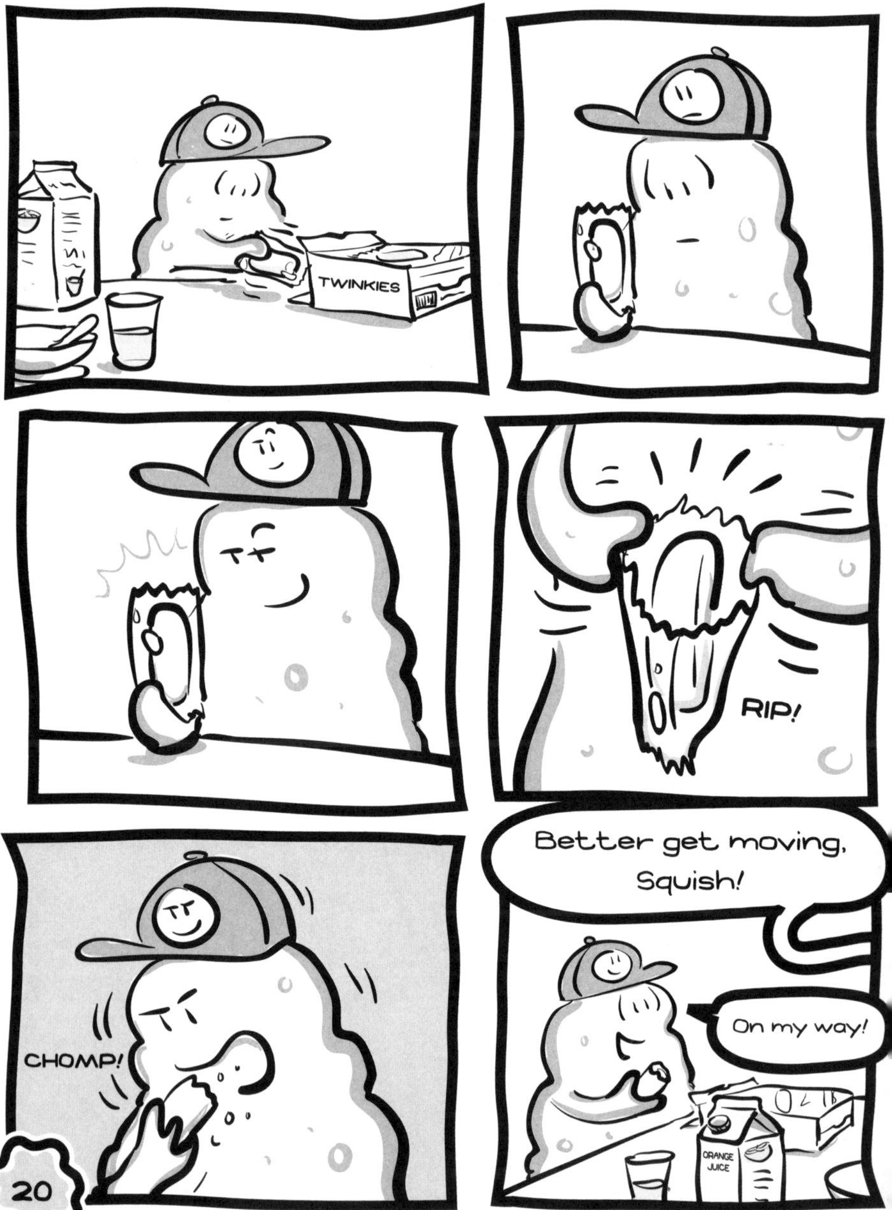
TWINKIES
RIP!
CHOMP!
Better get moving, Squish!
On my way!
ORANGE JUICE

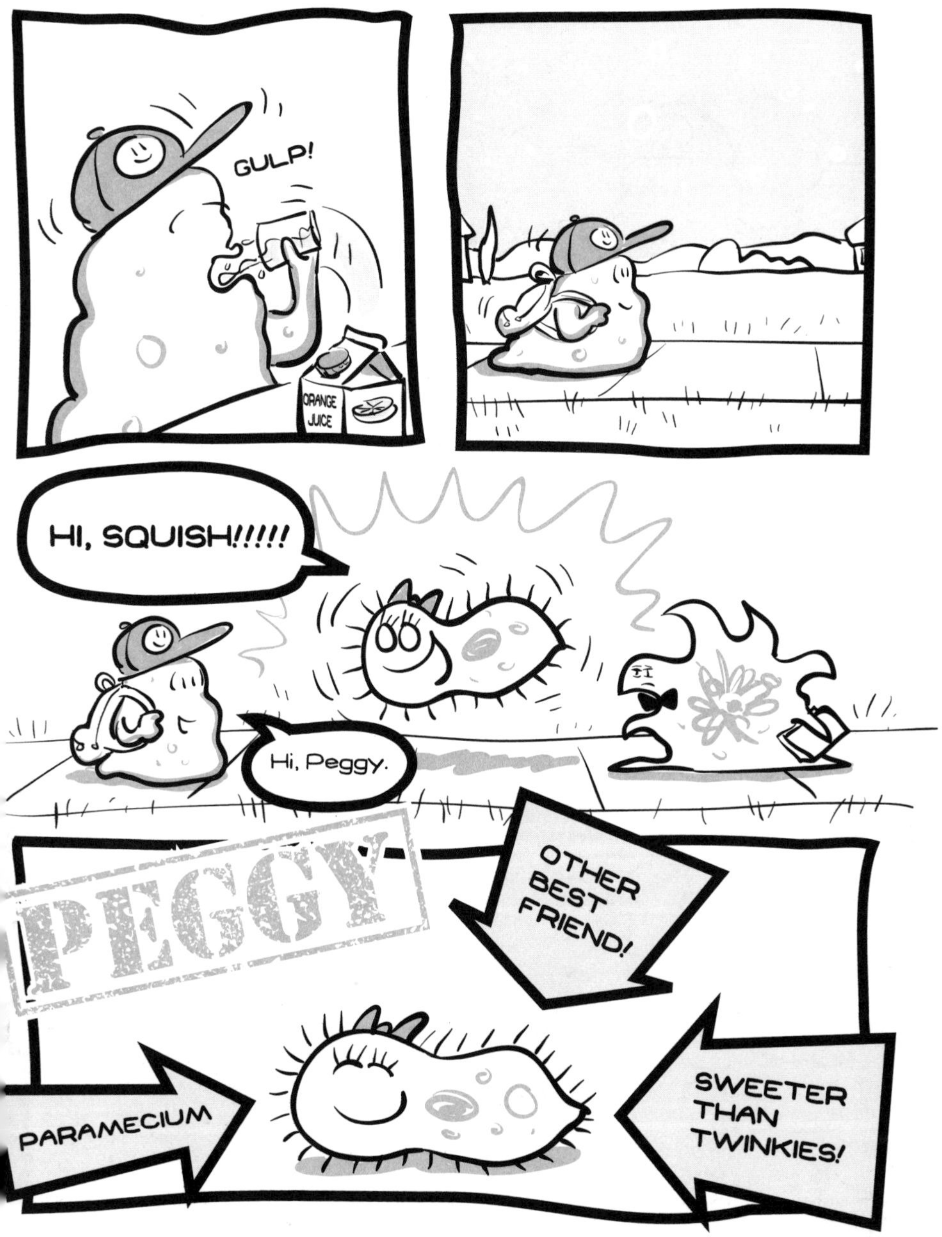
GULP!
ORANGE JUICE
HI, SQUISH!!!!!
Hi, Peggy.
PEGGY
OTHER BEST FRIEND!
PARAMECIUM
SWEETER THAN TWINKIES!

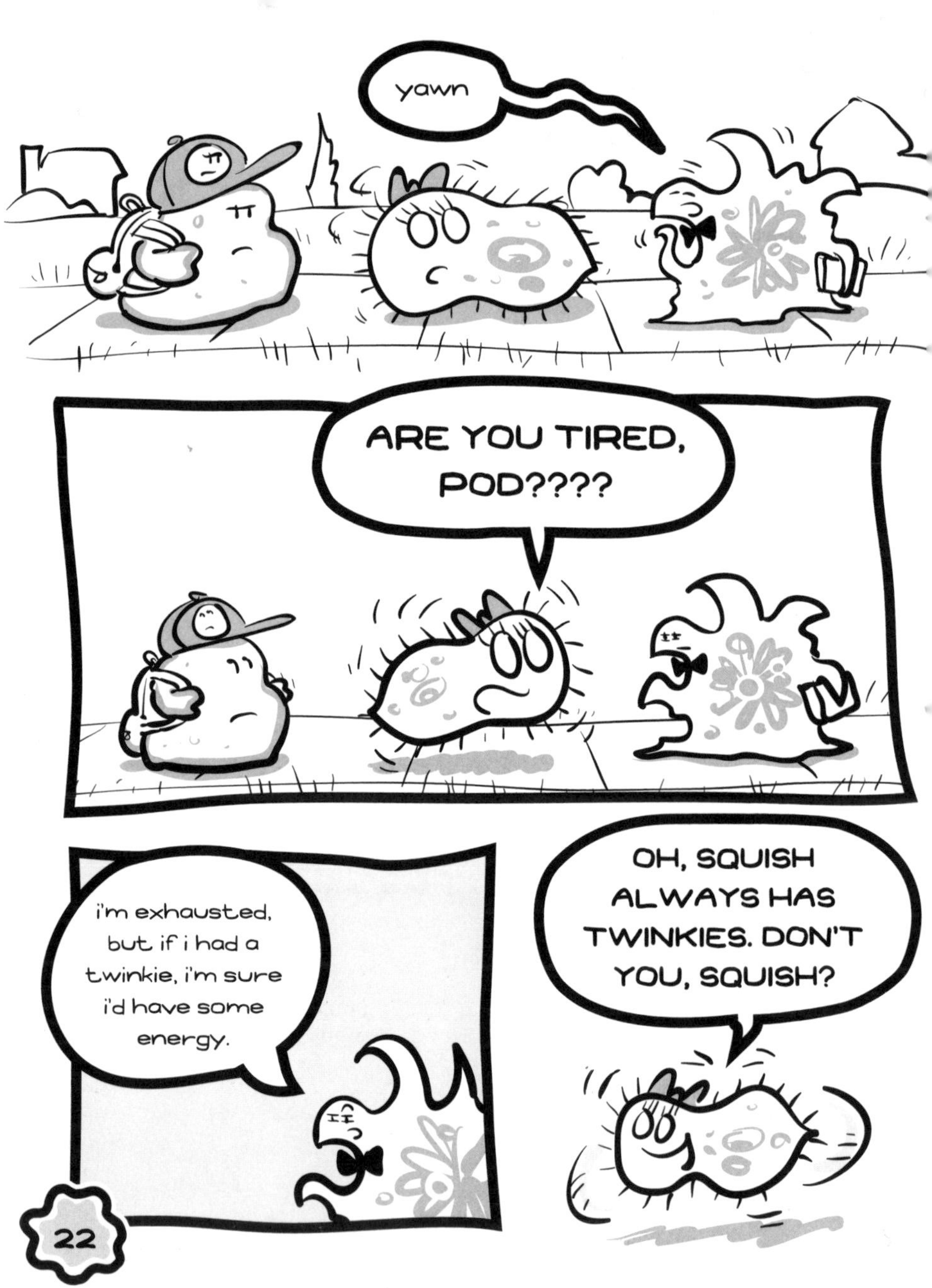
yawn
ARE YOU TIRED, POD????
i'm exhausted, but if i had a twinkie, i'm sure i'd have some energy.
OH, SQUISH ALWAYS HAS TWINKIES. DON'T YOU, SQUISH?

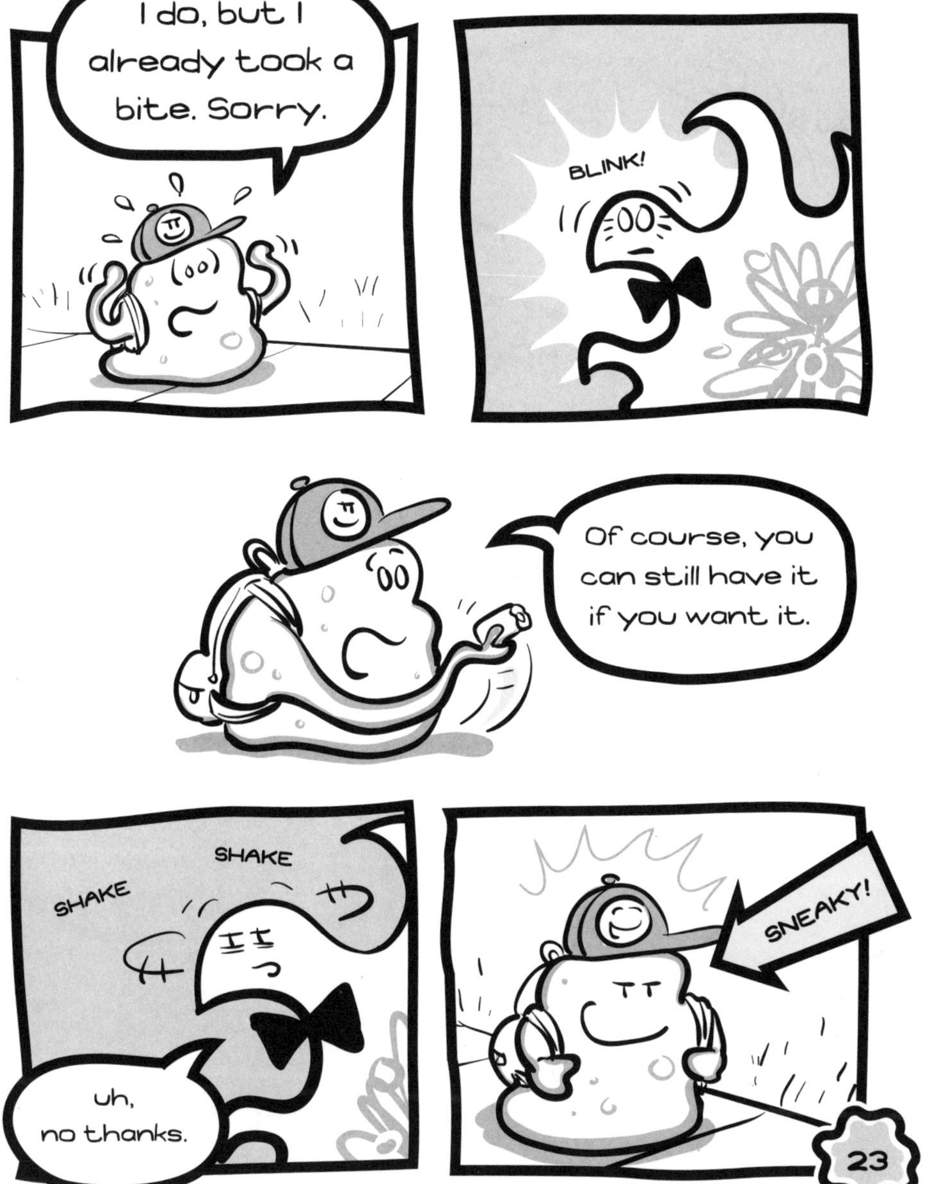
I do, but I already took a bite. Sorry.
BLINK!
Of course, you can still have it if you want it.
SHAKE
SHAKE
uh, no thanks.
SNEAKY!

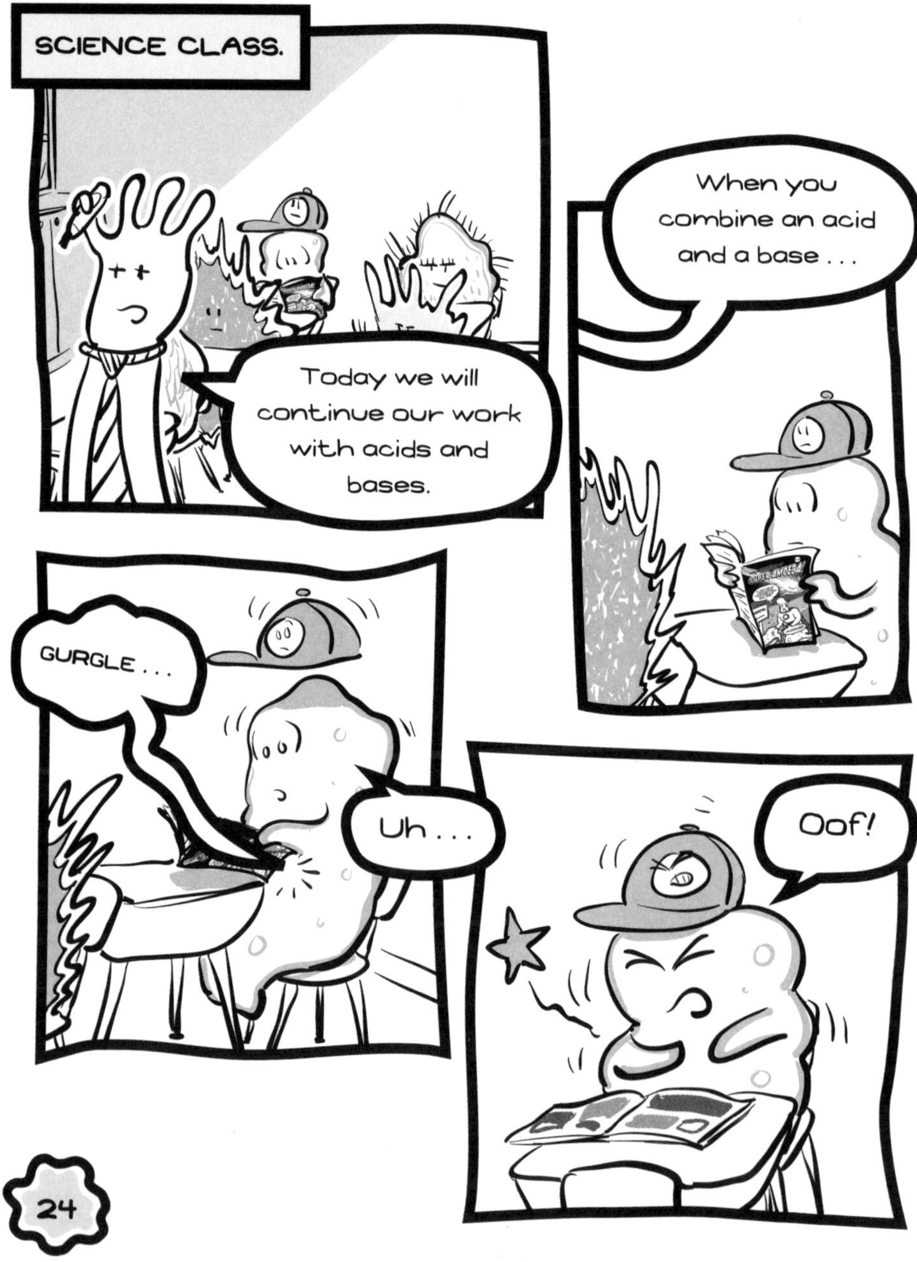
SCIENCE CLASS.
Today we will continue our work with acids and bases.
When you combine an acid and a base . . .
GURGLE . . .
Uh . . .
Oof!

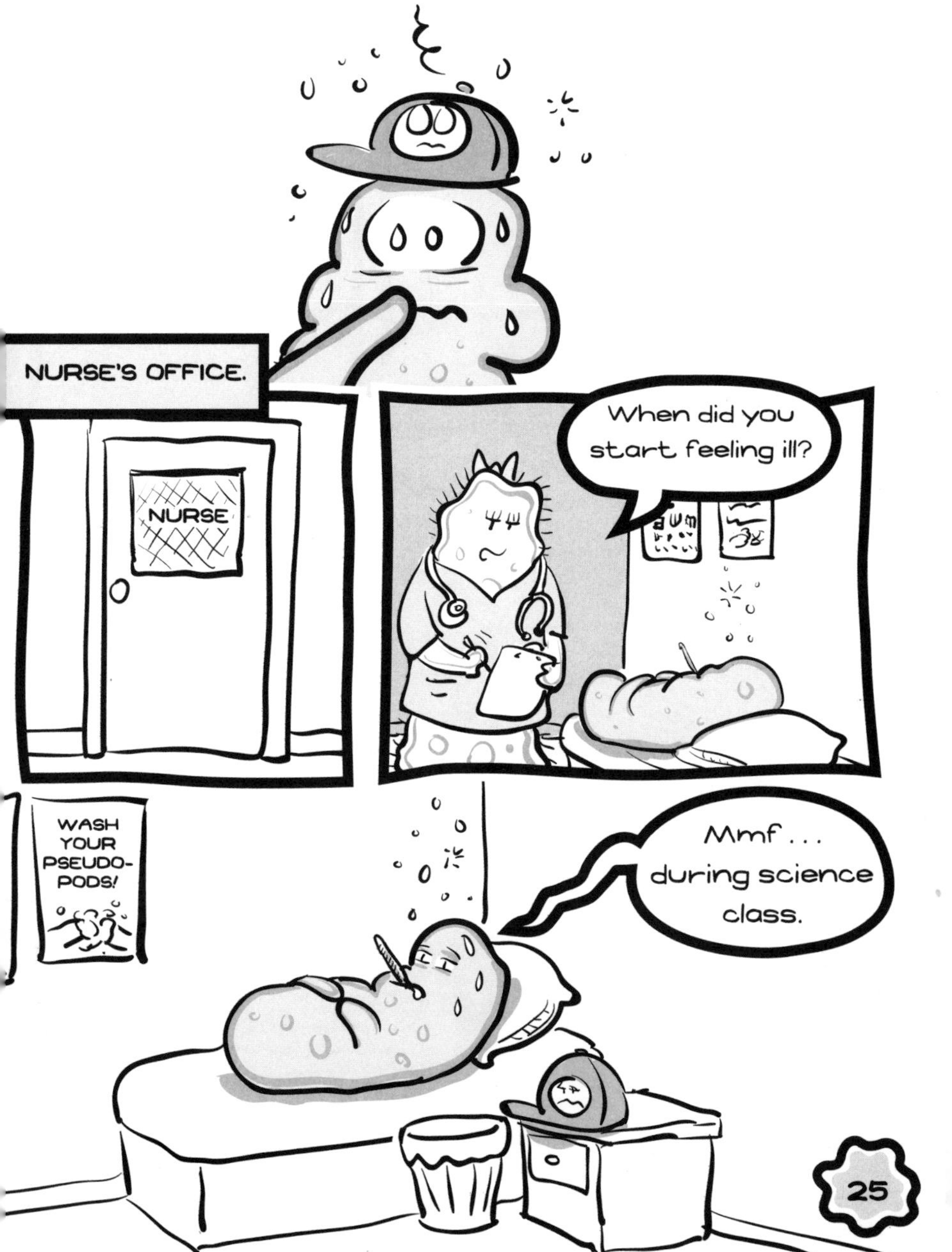

NURSE'S OFFICE.
NURSE
When did you start feeling ill?
WASH YOUR PSEUDO-PODS!
Mmf . . . during science class.

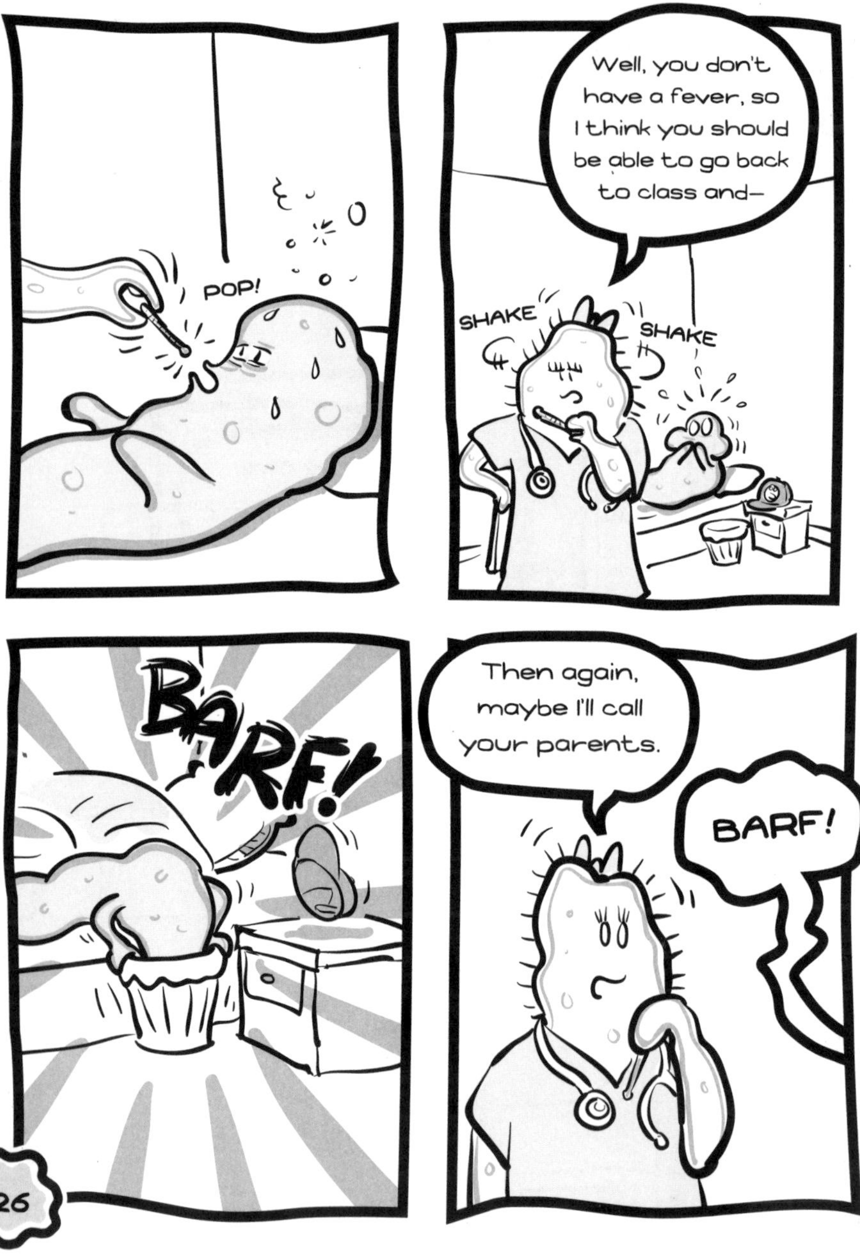
POP!
Well, you don't have a fever, so I think you should be able to go back to class and–
SHAKE
SHAKE
BARF!
Then again, maybe I'll call your parents.
BARF!

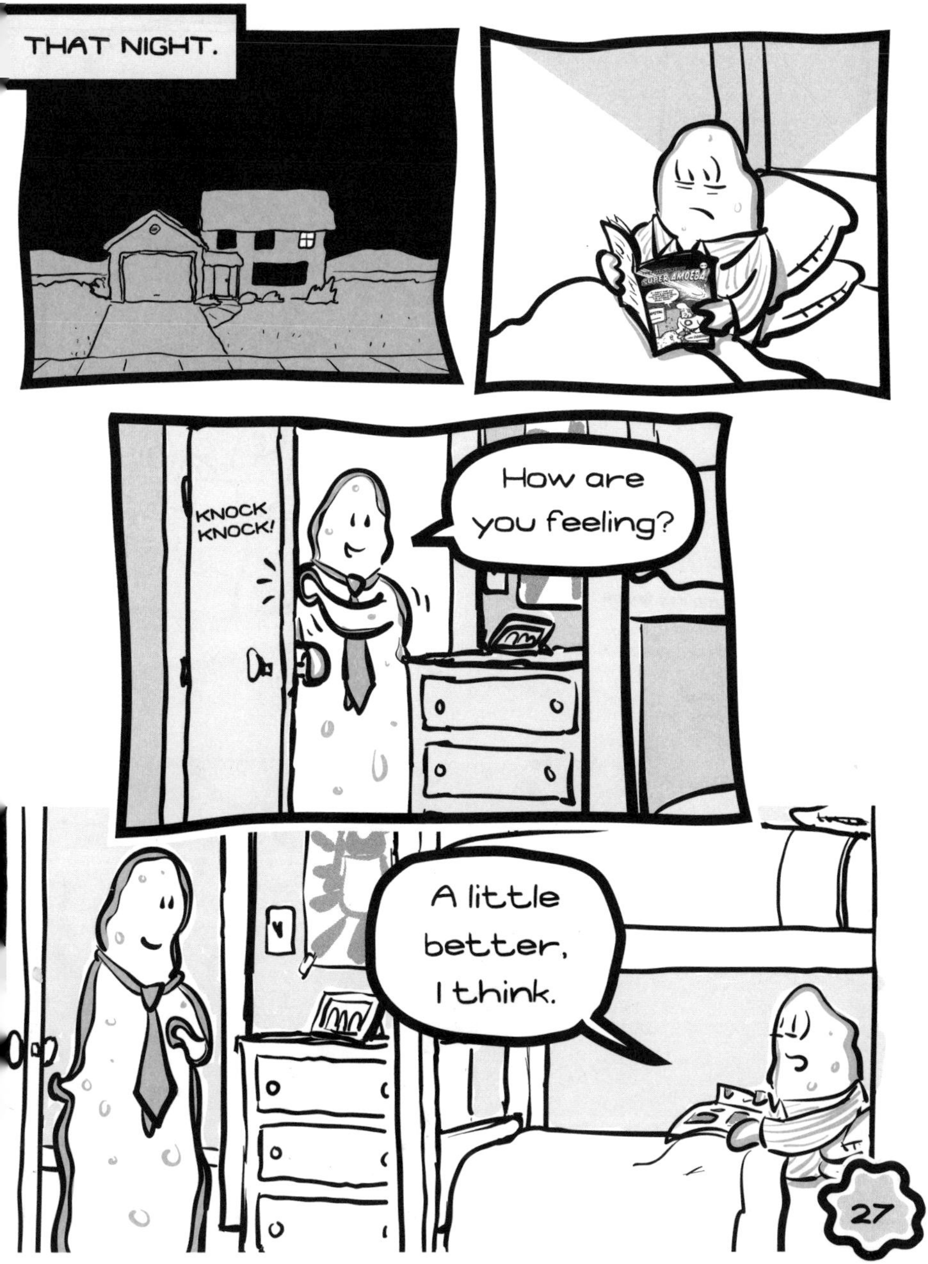

THAT NIGHT.
SUPER AMOEBA
KNOCK KNOCK!
How are you feeling?
A little better, I think.
27

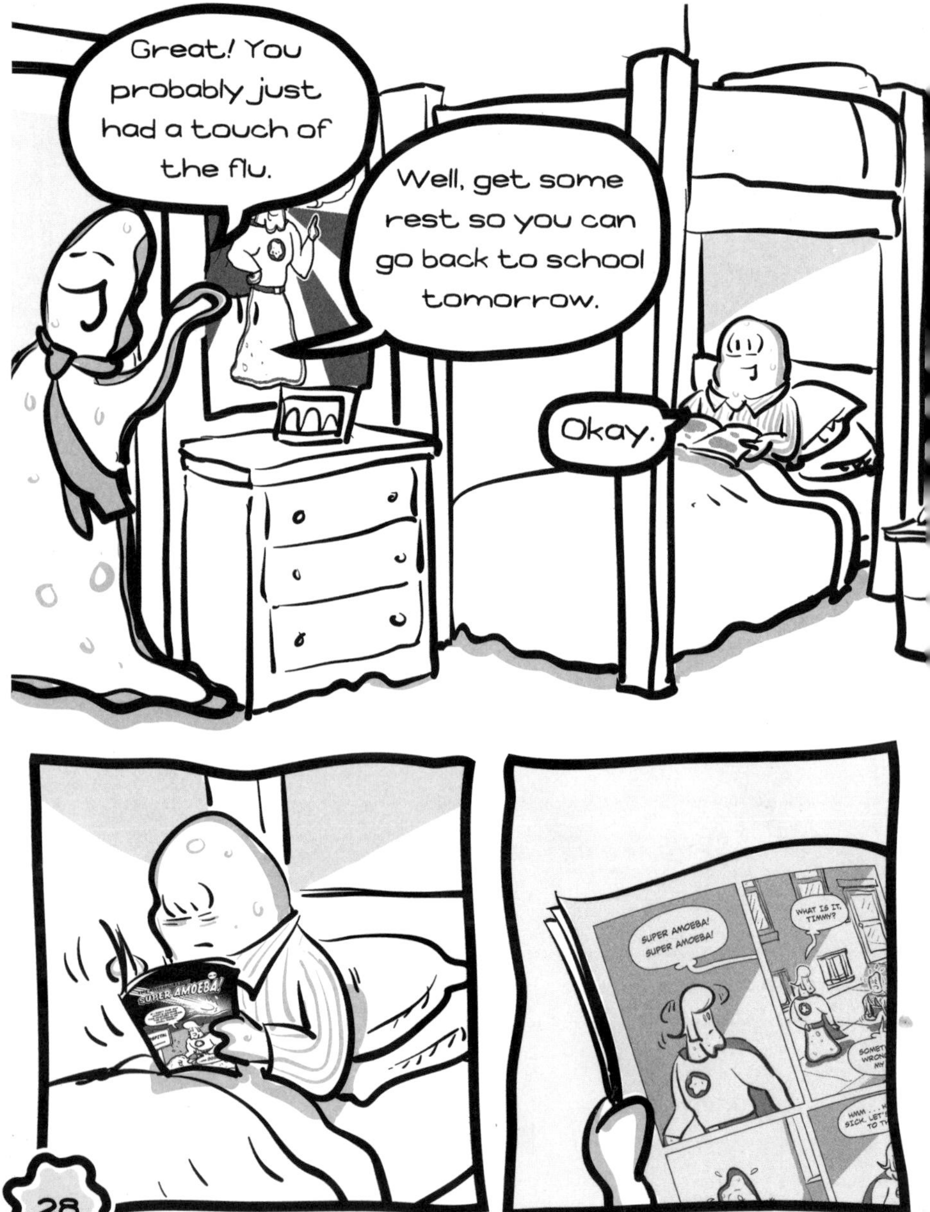
Great! You probably just had a touch of the flu.
Well, get some rest so you can go back to school tomorrow.
Okay.
SUPER AMOEBA!
SUPER AMOEBA! SUPER AMOEBA!
WHAT IS IT, TIMMY?

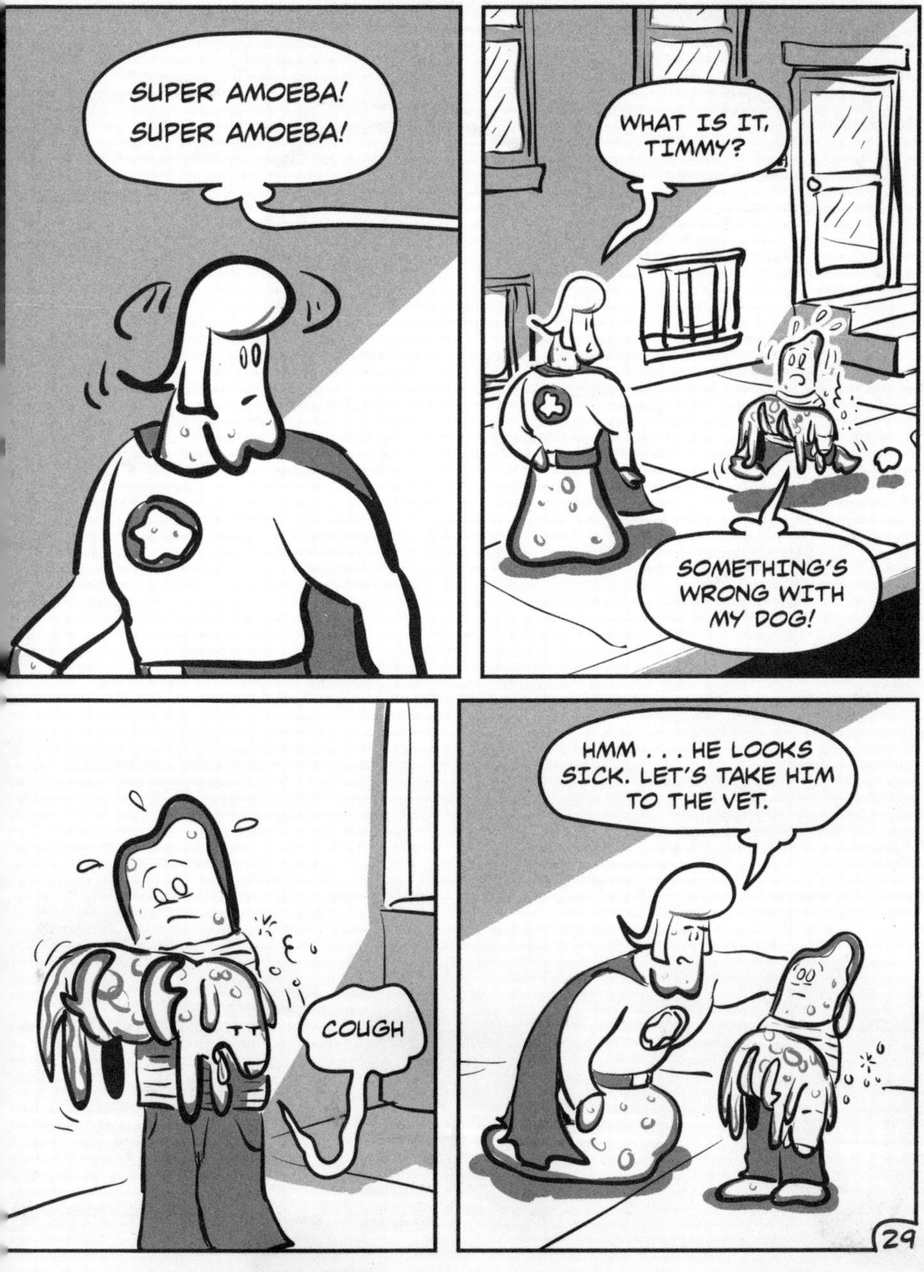
SUPER AMOEBA!
SUPER AMOEBA!
WHAT IS IT, TIMMY?
SOMETHING'S WRONG WITH MY DOG!
COUGH
HMM . . . HE LOOKS SICK. LET'S TAKE HIM TO THE VET.

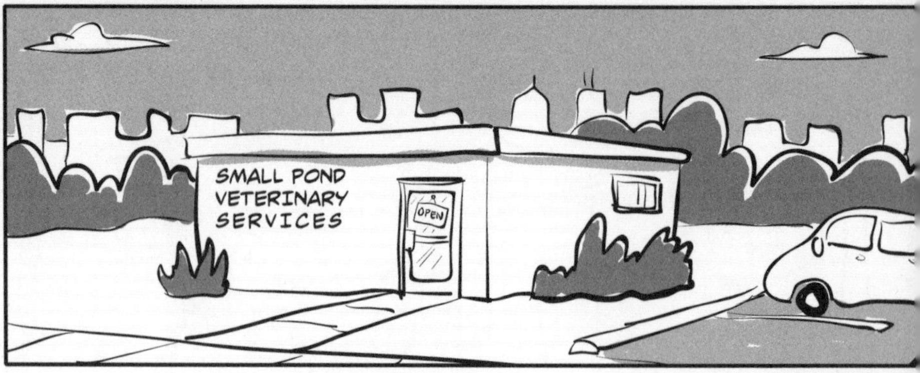
SMALL POND
VETERINARY
SERVICES
OPEN

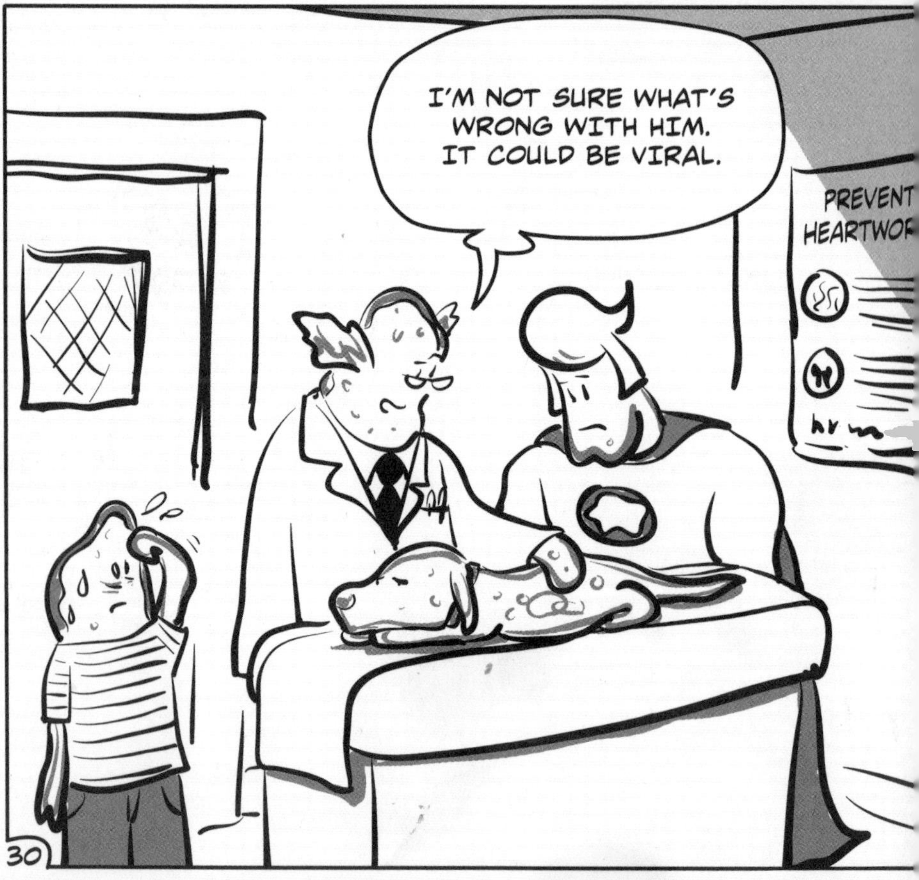
I'M NOT SURE WHAT'S WRONG WITH HIM. IT COULD BE VIRAL.
PREVENT
HEARTWOR

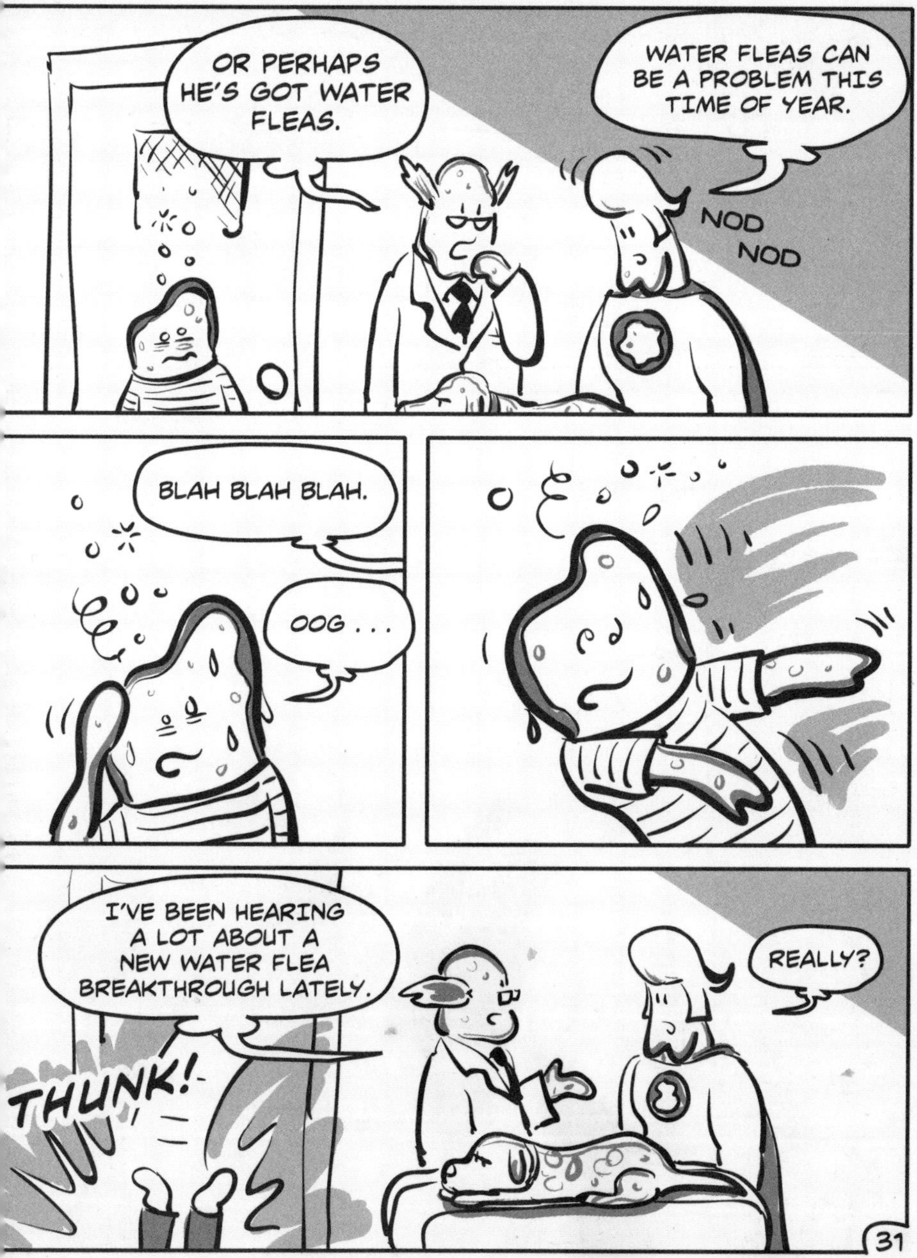
OR PERHAPS HE'S GOT WATER FLEAS.
WATER FLEAS CAN BE A PROBLEM THIS TIME OF YEAR.
NOD NOD
BLAH BLAH BLAH.
OOG . . .
I'VE BEEN HEARING A LOT ABOUT A NEW WATER FLEA BREAKTHROUGH LATELY.
REALLY?
THUNK!

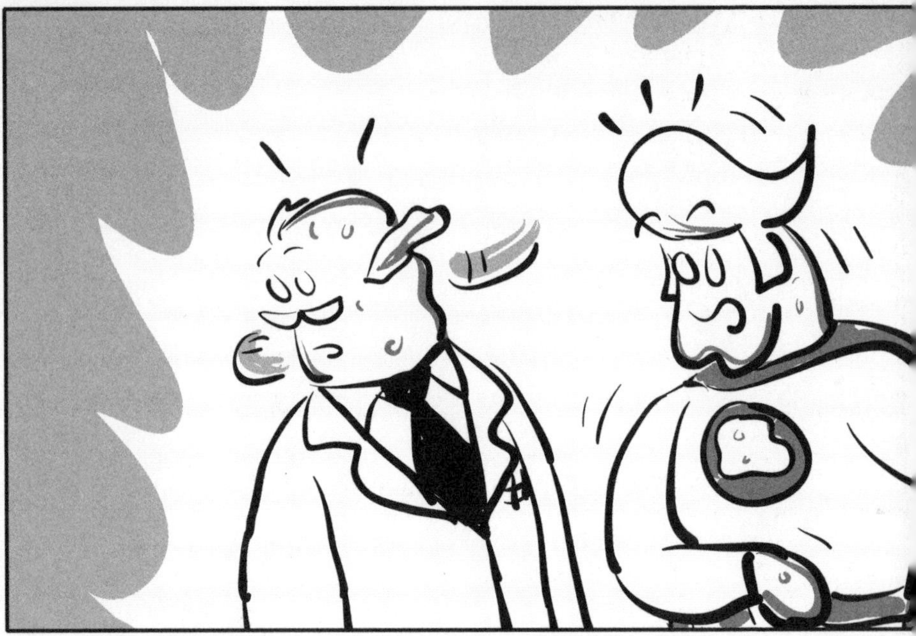

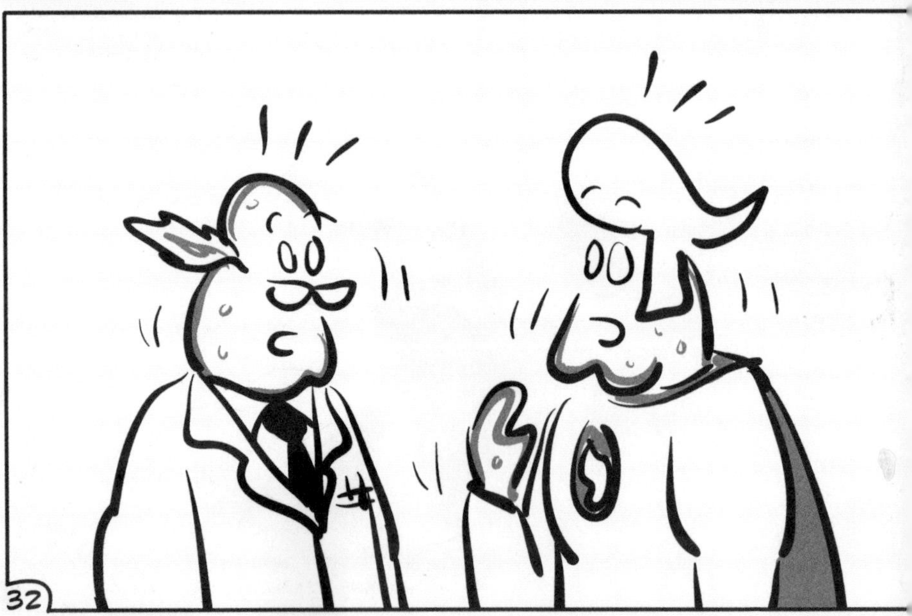

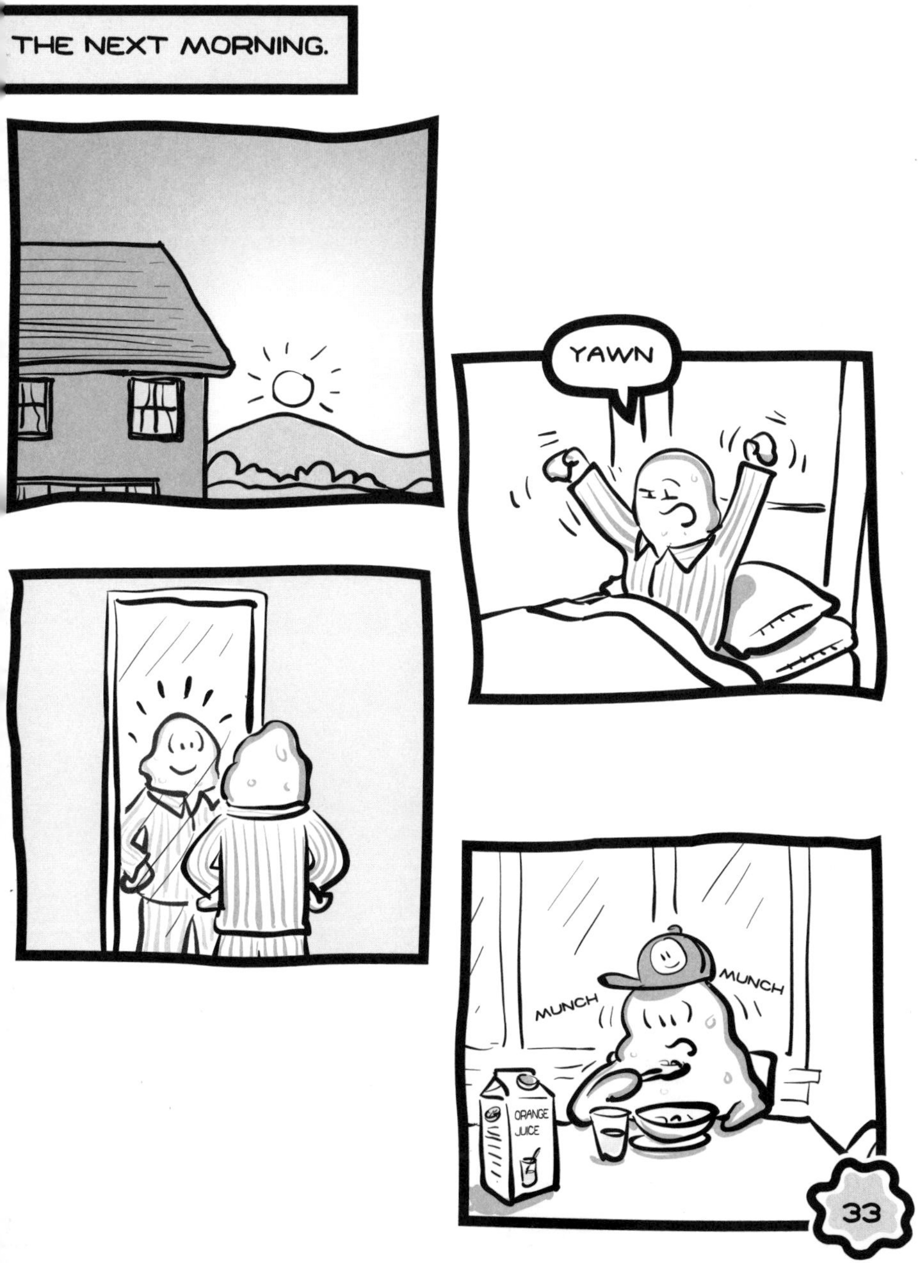
THE NEXT MORNING.
YAWN
MUNCH
MUNCH
ORANGE JUICE

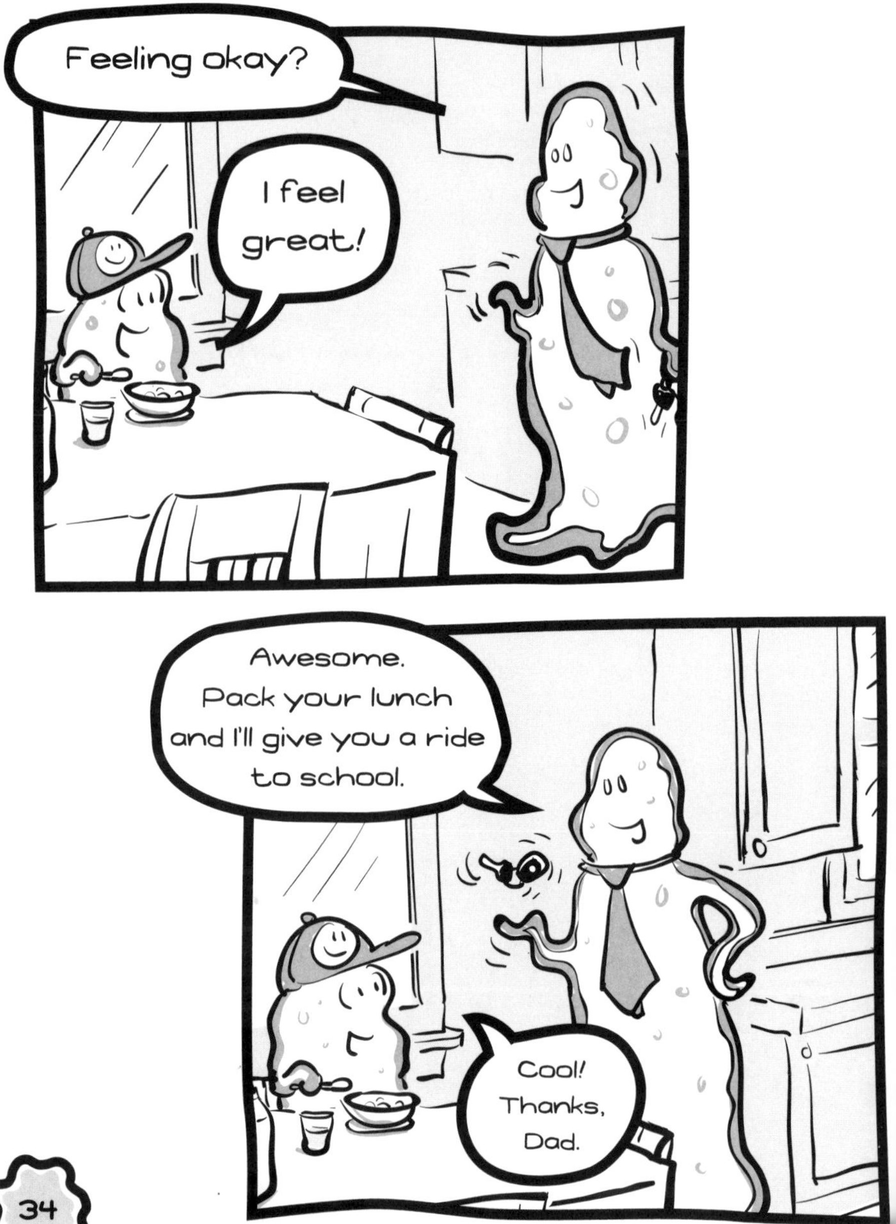
Feeling okay?
I feel great!
Awesome. Pack your lunch and I'll give you a ride to school.
Cool! Thanks, Dad.

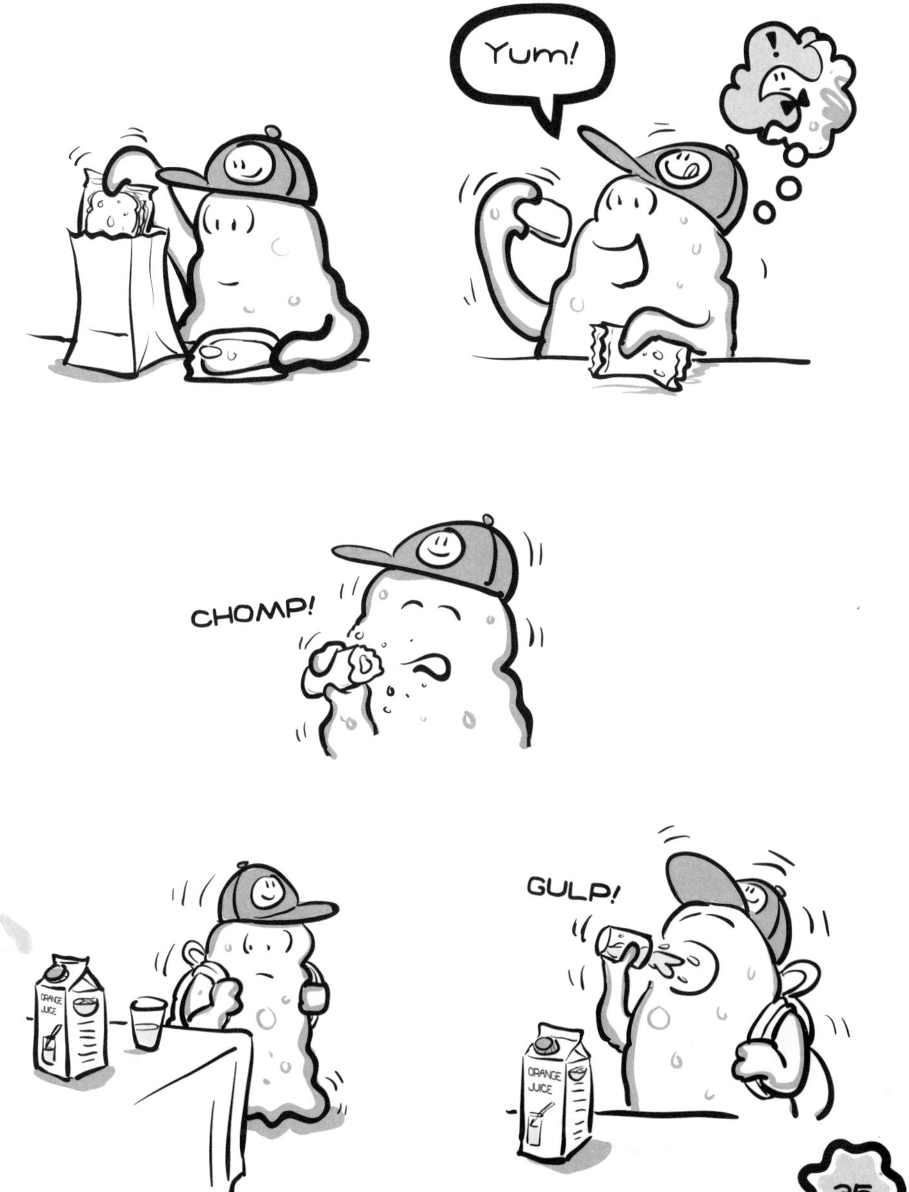
Yum!
CHOMP!
ORANGE JUICE
GULP!
ORANGE JUICE

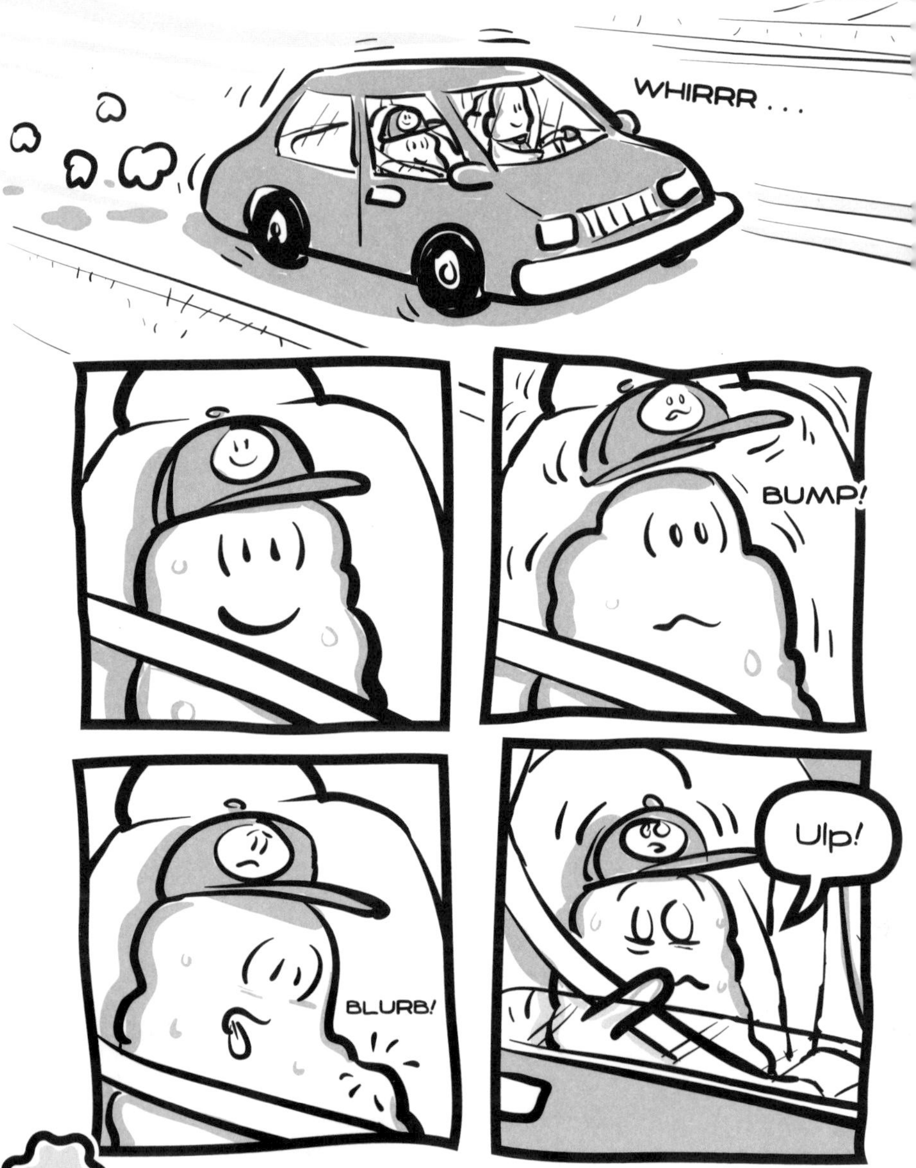
WHIRRR . . .
BUMP!
BLURB!
Ulp!

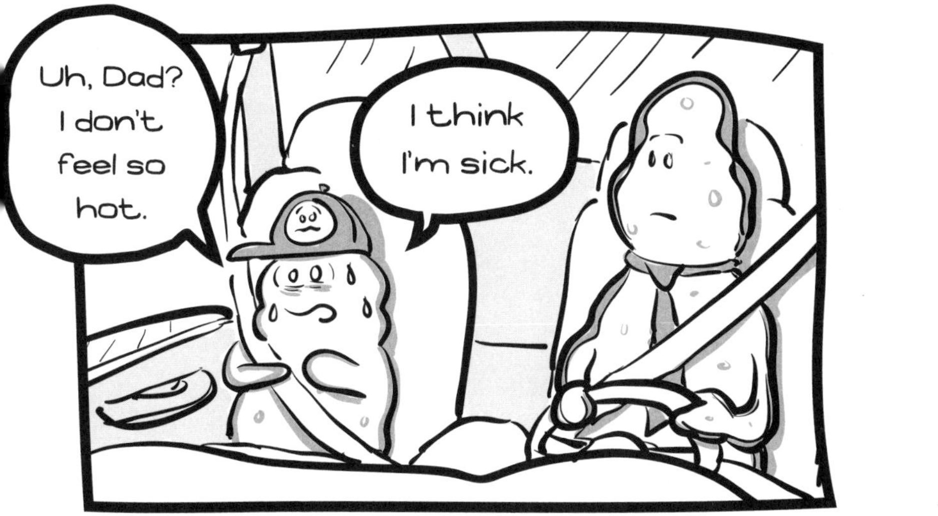
Uh, Dad? I don't feel so hot.
I think I'm sick.

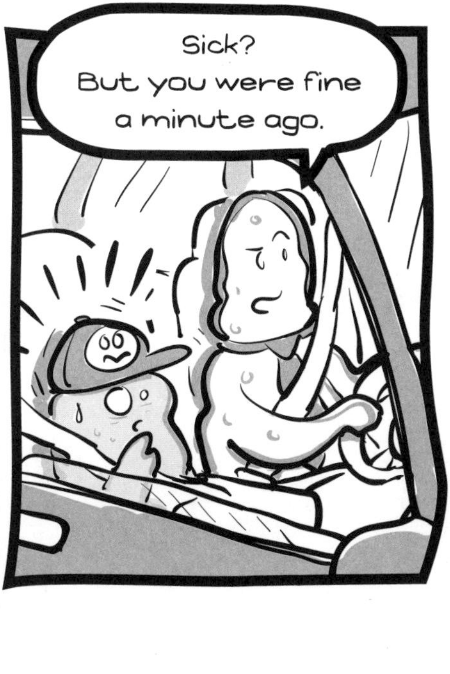
Sick? But you were fine a minute ago.

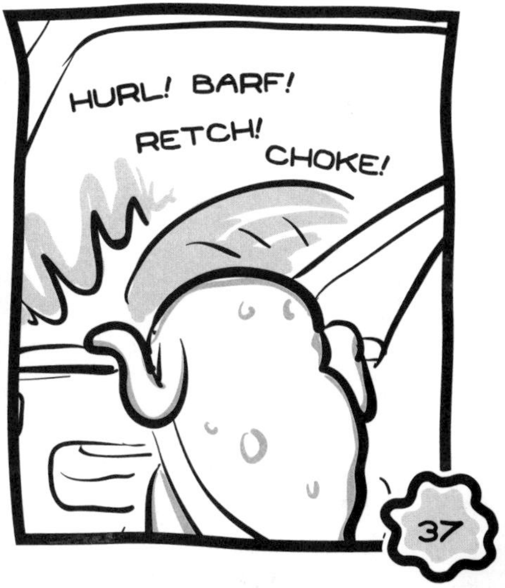
HURL! BARF!
RETCH!
CHOKE!

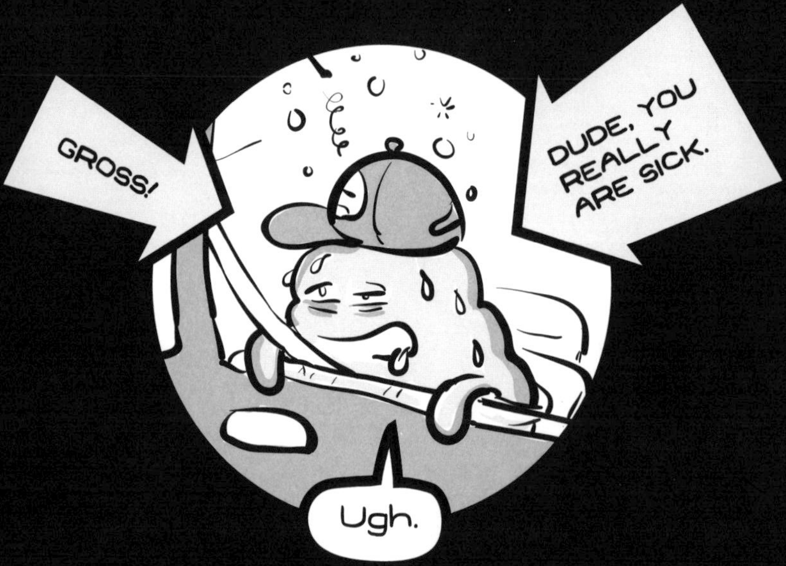
GROSS!
DUDE, YOU REALLY ARE SICK.
Ugh.

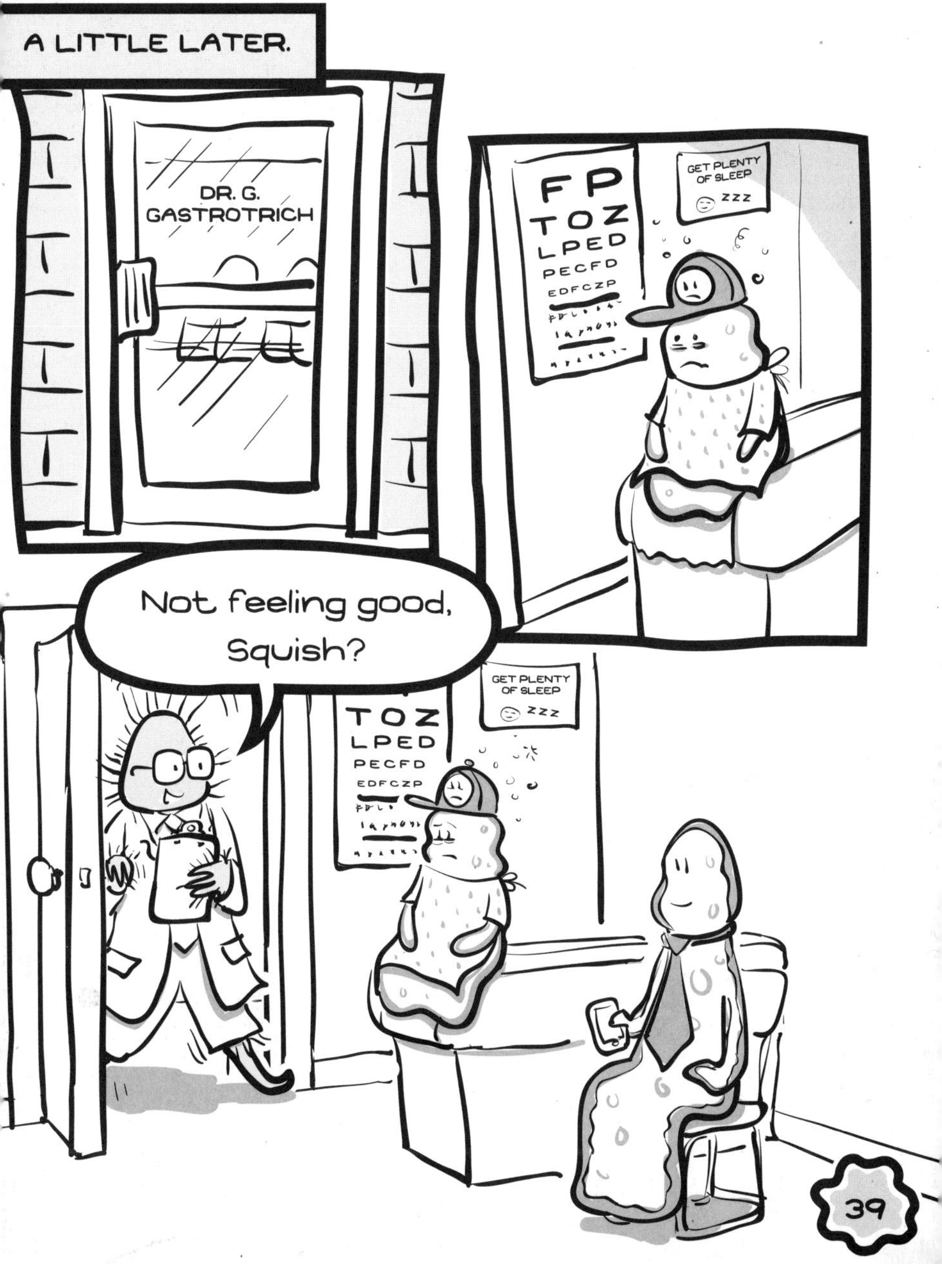

A LITTLE LATER.
DR. G. GASTROTRICH
FPTOZLPEDPECFDEDFCZP
GET PLENTY OF SLEEP
ZZZ
Not feeling good, Squish?
TOZLPEDPECFDEDFCZP
GET PLENTY OF SLEEP
ZZZ

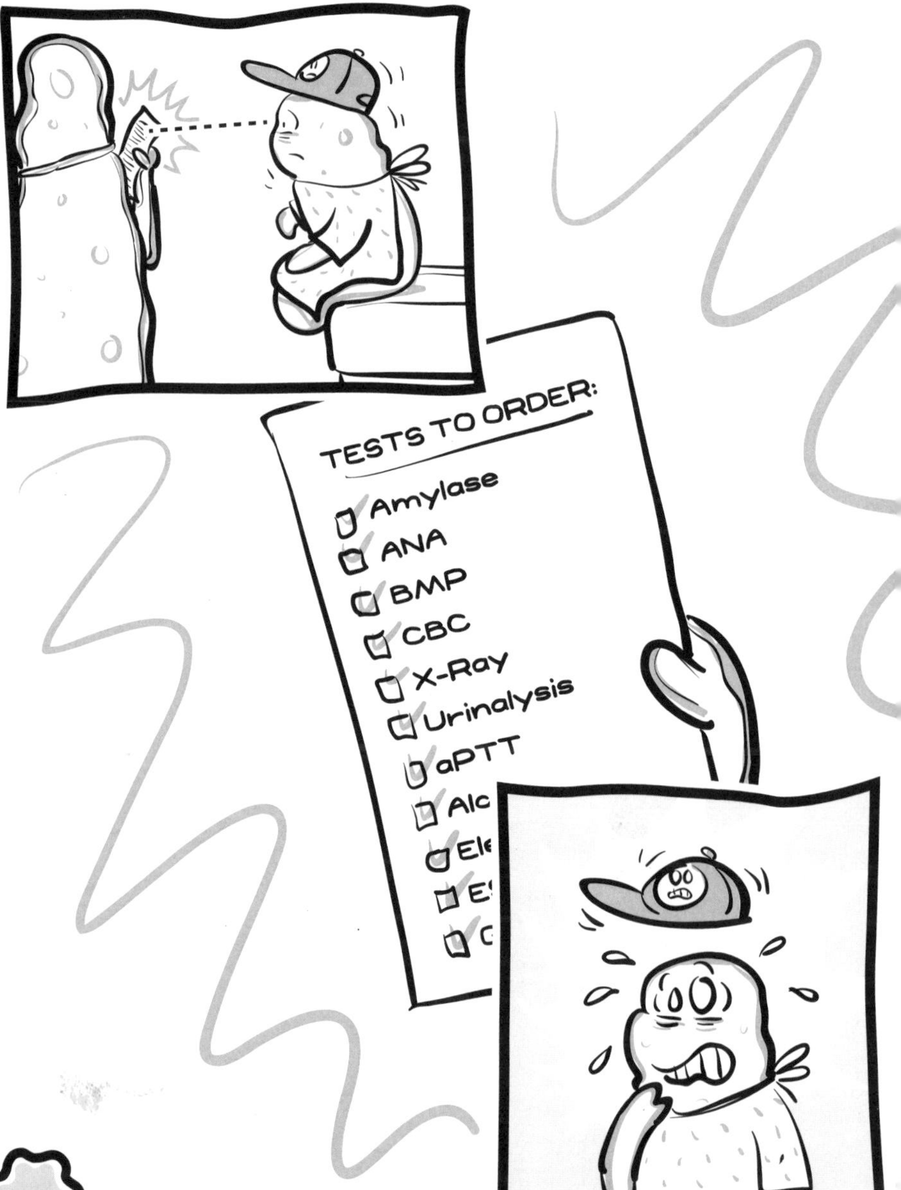
TESTS TO ORDER:
Amylase
ANA
BMP
CBC
X-Ray
Urinalysis
aPTT
Alc
Ele

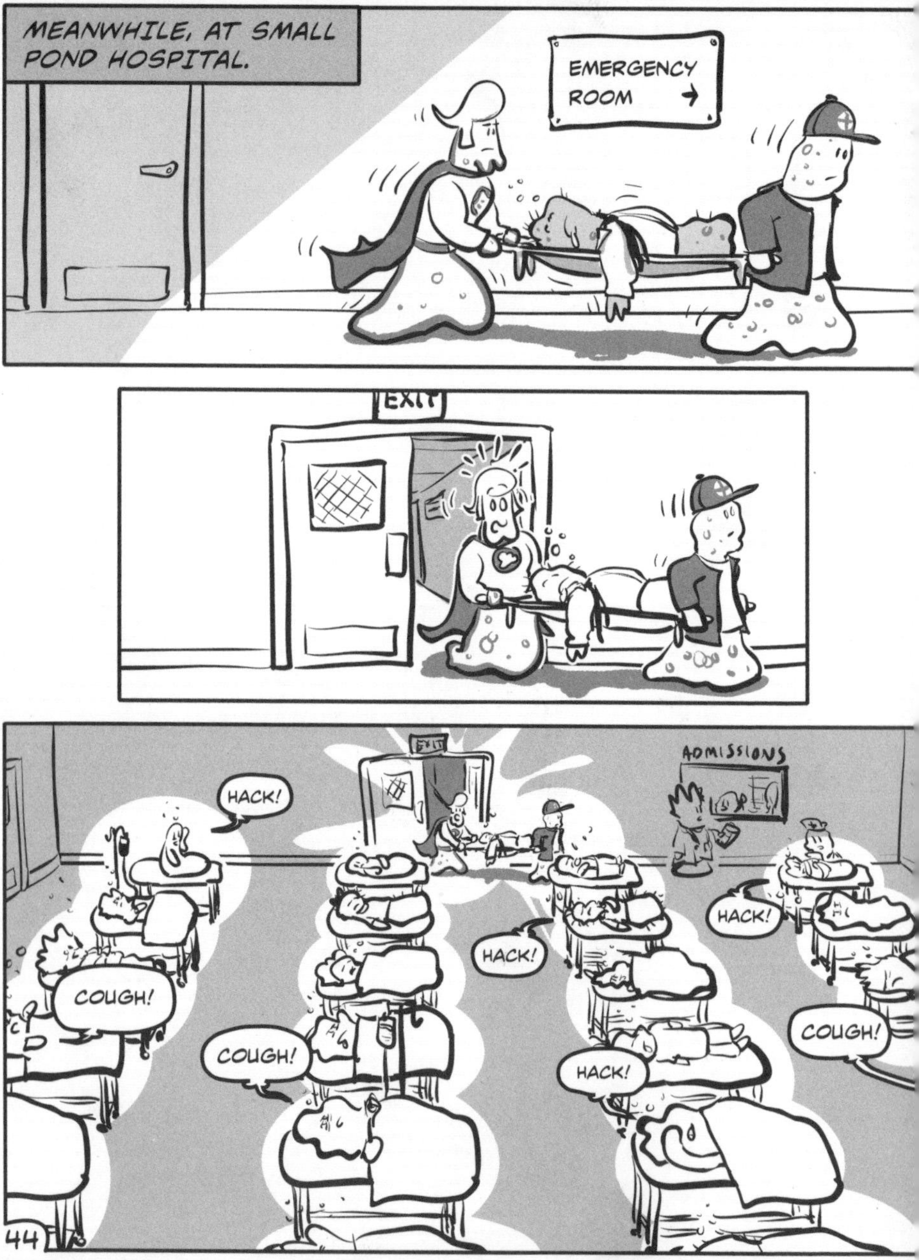
MEANWHILE, AT SMALL POND HOSPITAL.
EMERGENCY ROOM →
EXIT
EXIT
ADMISSIONS
HACK!
HACK!
HACK!
COUGH!
COUGH!
HACK!
COUGH!

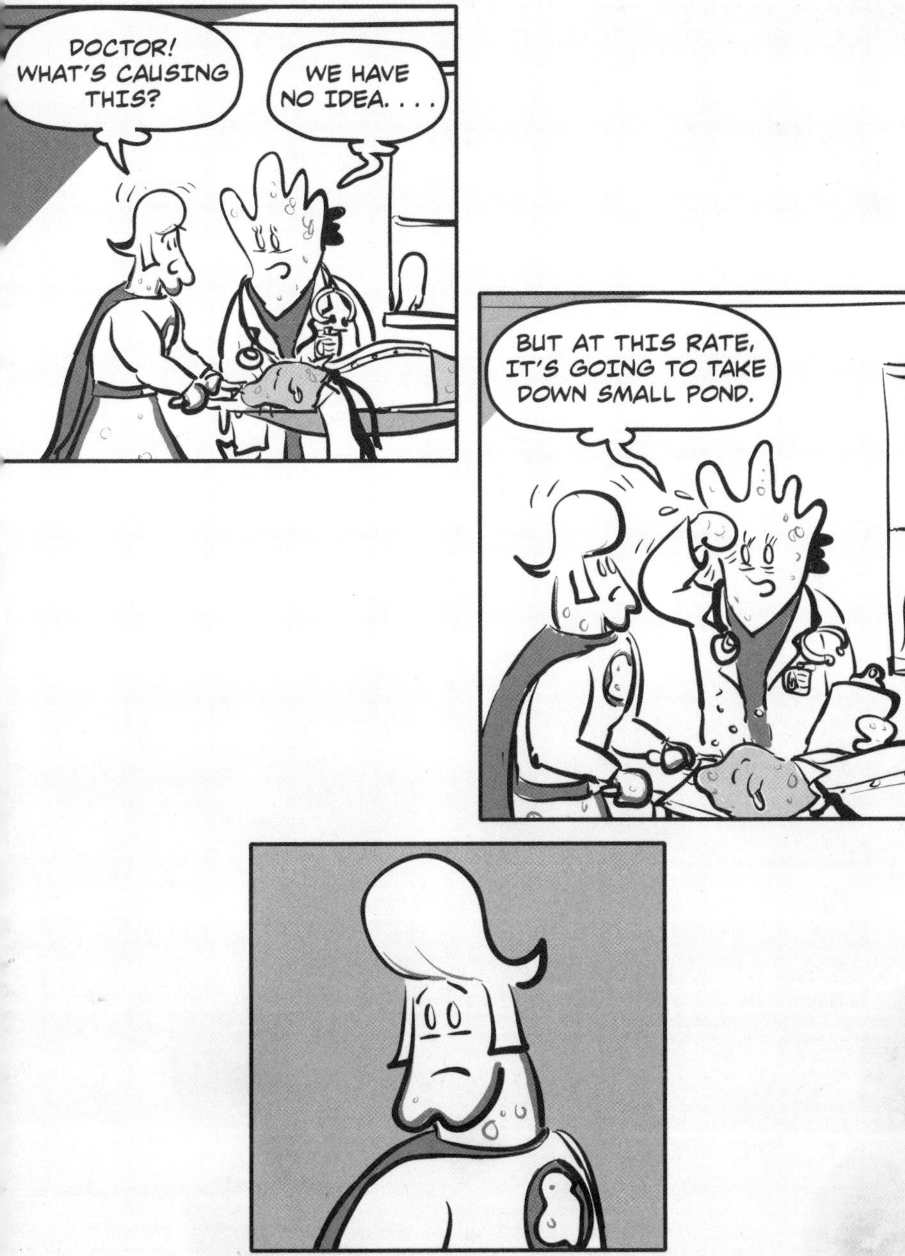
DOCTOR! WHAT'S CAUSING THIS?
WE HAVE NO IDEA. . . .
BUT AT THIS RATE, IT'S GOING TO TAKE DOWN SMALL POND.

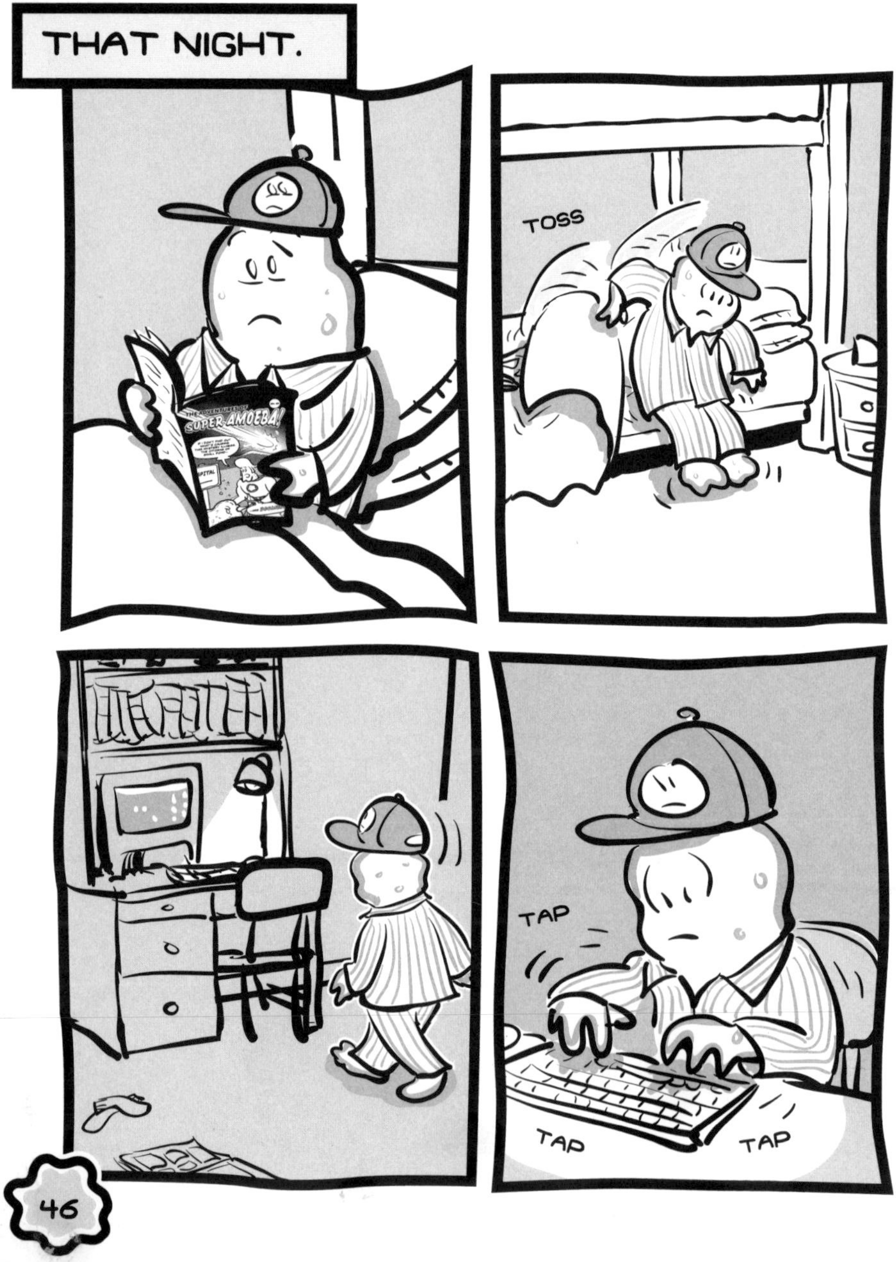
THAT NIGHT.
THE ADVENTURES OF SUPER-AMOEBA!
TOSS
TAP
TAP
TAP

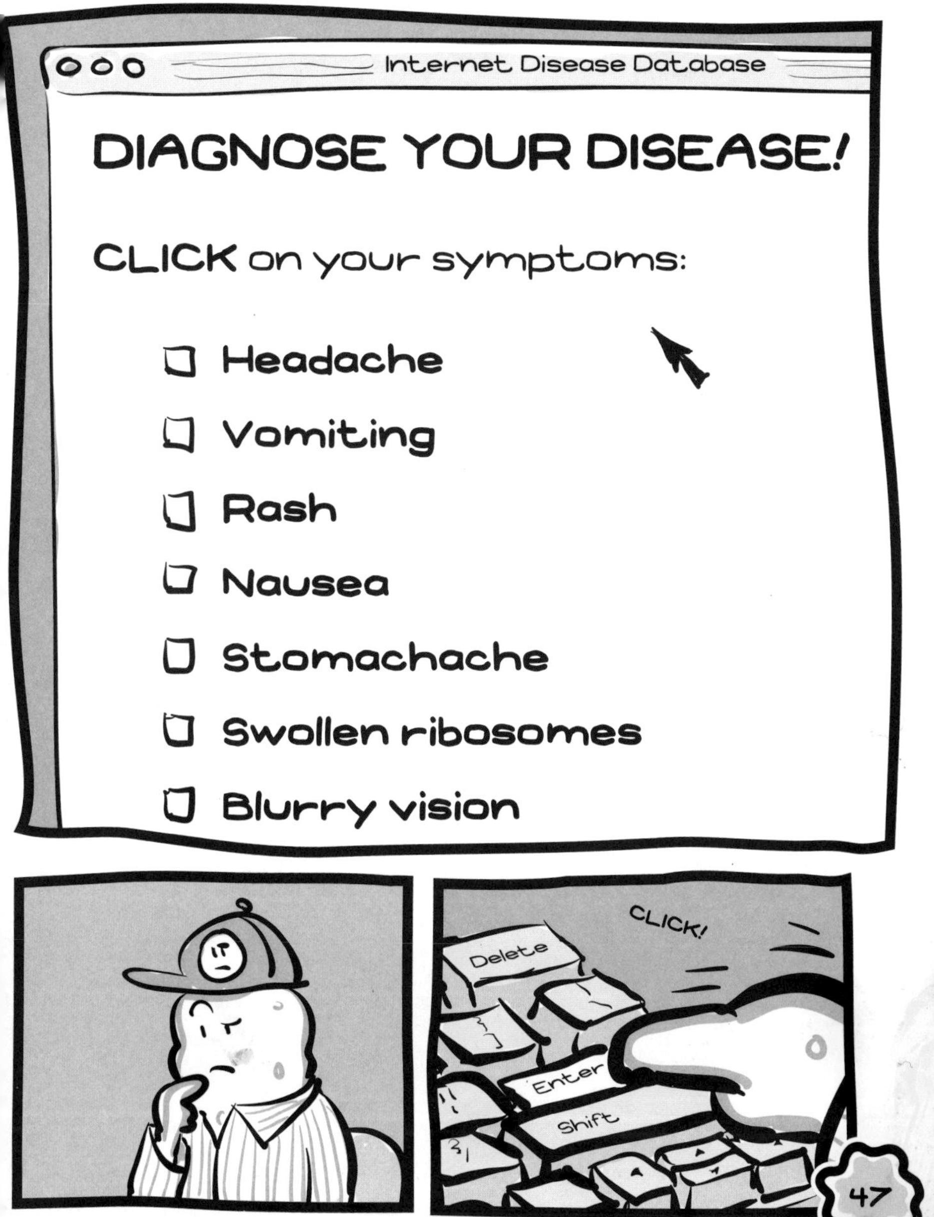
Internet Disease Database
DIAGNOSE YOUR DISEASE!
CLICK on your symptoms:
Headache
Vomiting
Rash
Nausea
Stomachache
Swollen ribosomes
Blurry vision
CLICK!
Delete
Enter
Shift

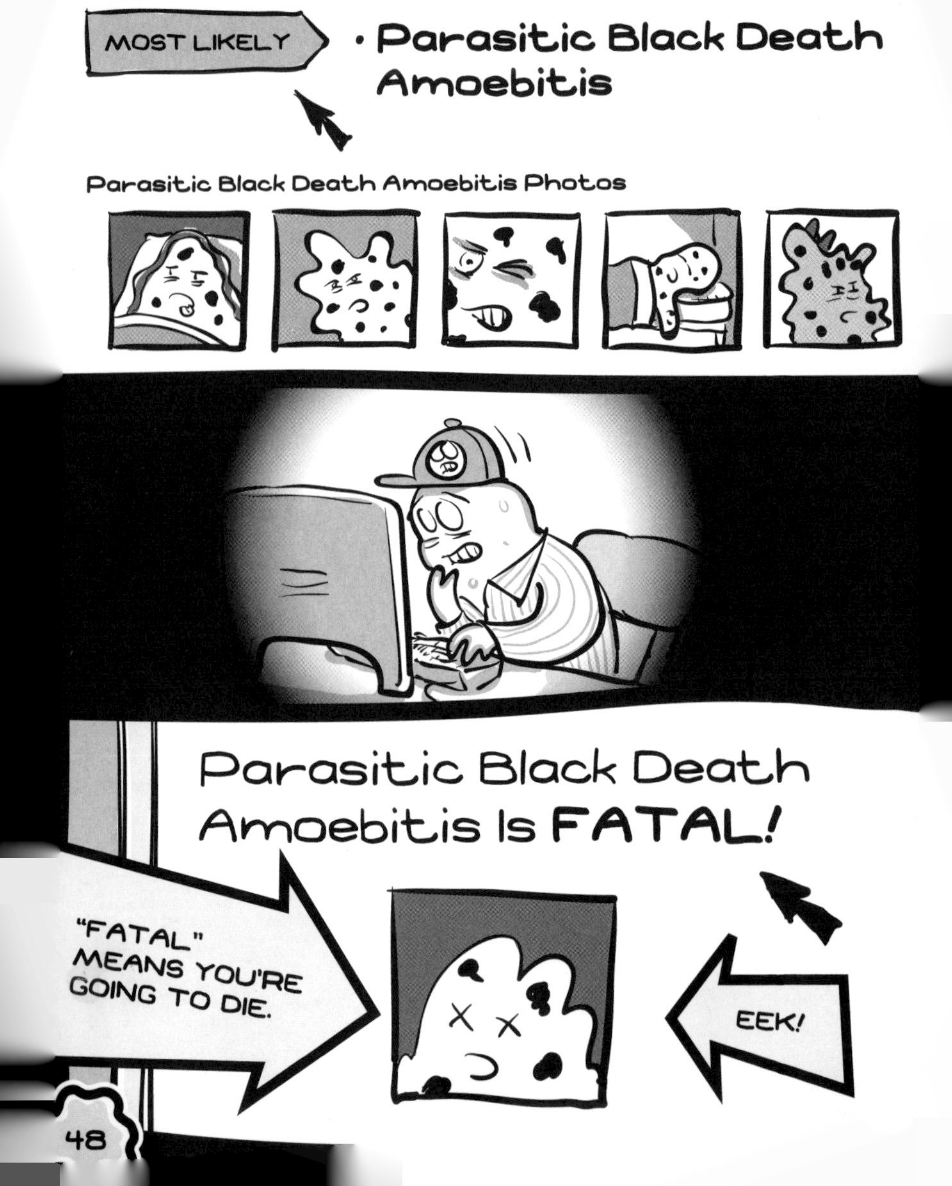
MOST LIKELY
• Parasitic Black Death Amoebitis
Parasitic Black Death Amoebitis Photos
Parasitic Black Death Amoebitis Is FATAL!
"FATAL" MEANS YOU'RE GOING TO DIE.
EEK!

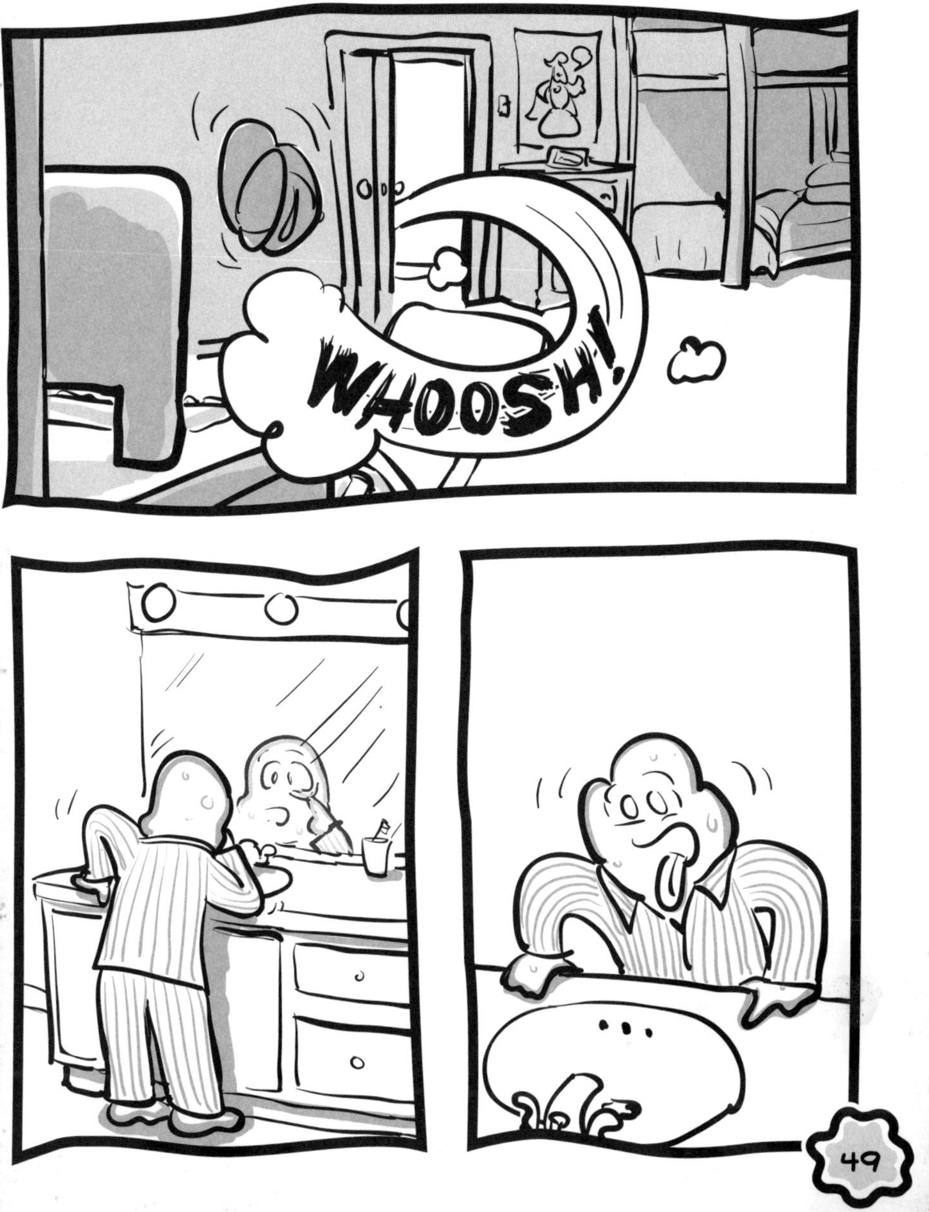
WHOOSH!

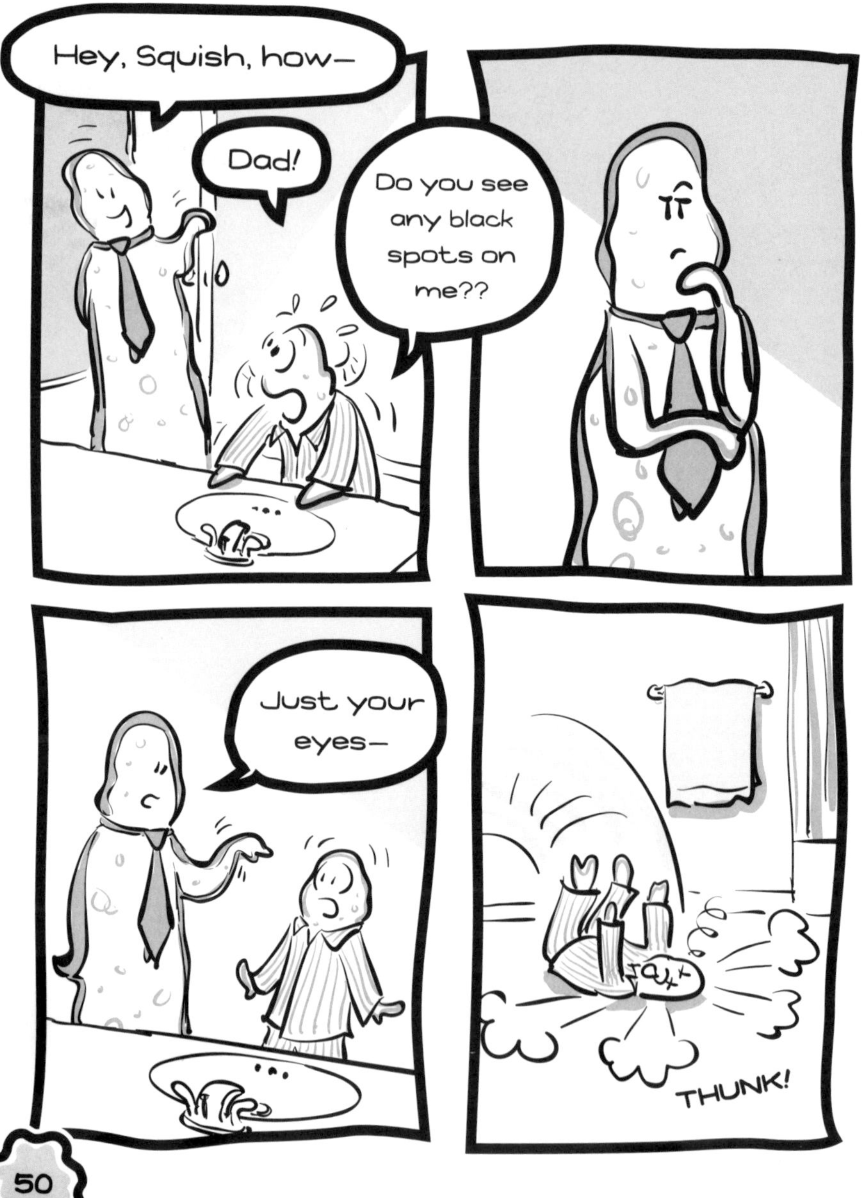
Hey, Squish, how—
Dad!
Do you see any black spots on me??
Just your eyes—
THUNK!

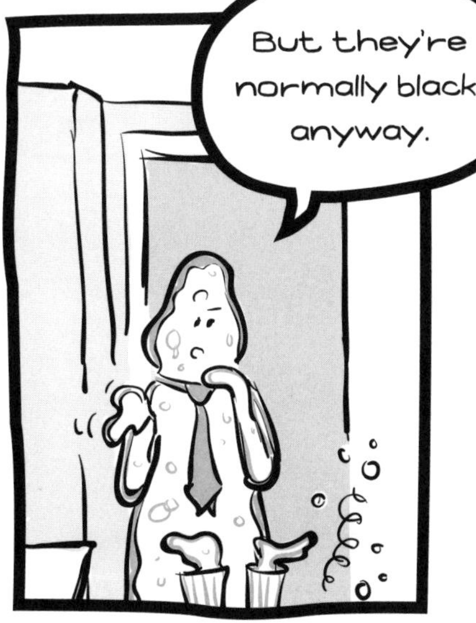
But they're normally black, anyway.

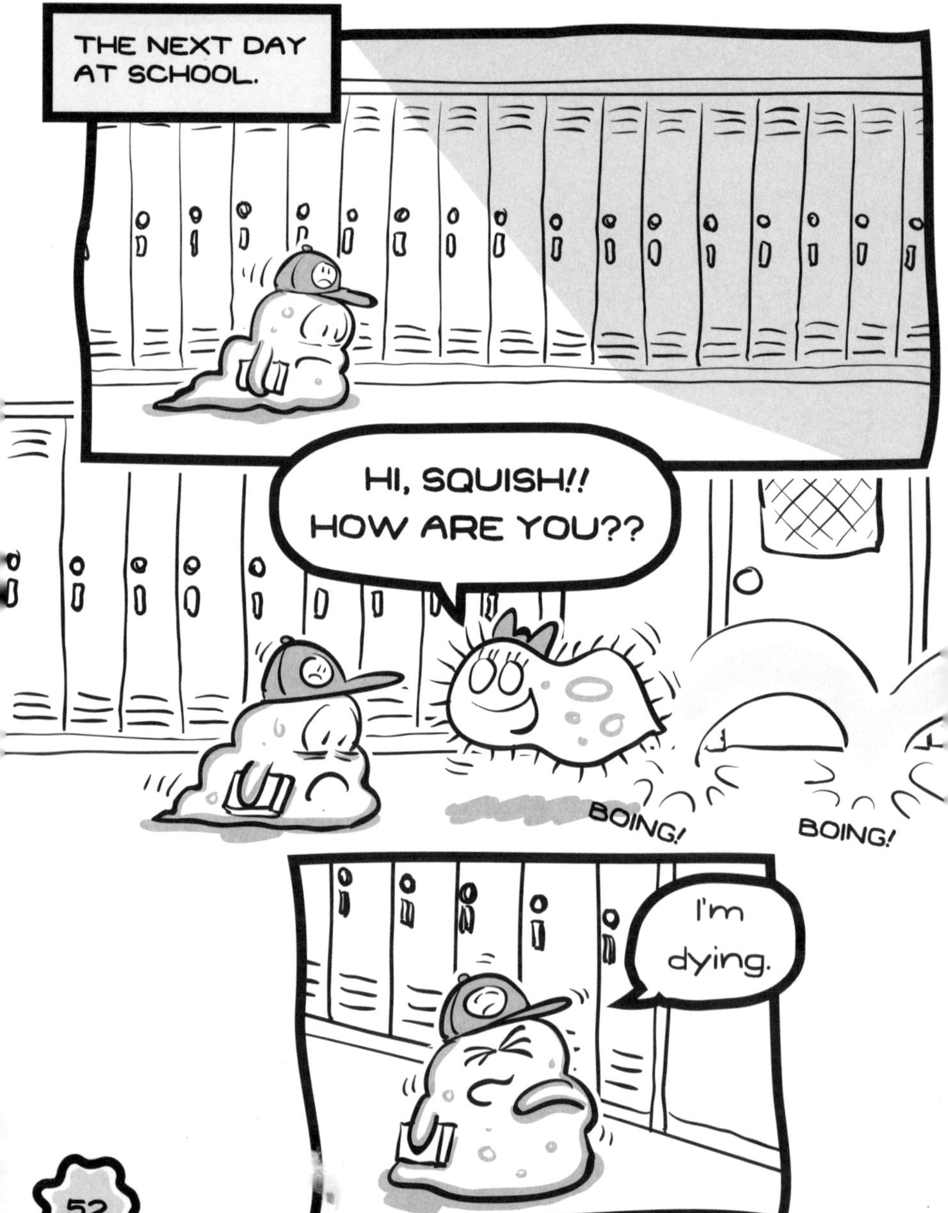
THE NEXT DAY AT SCHOOL.
HI, SQUISH!! HOW ARE YOU??
BOING!
BOING!
I'm dying.

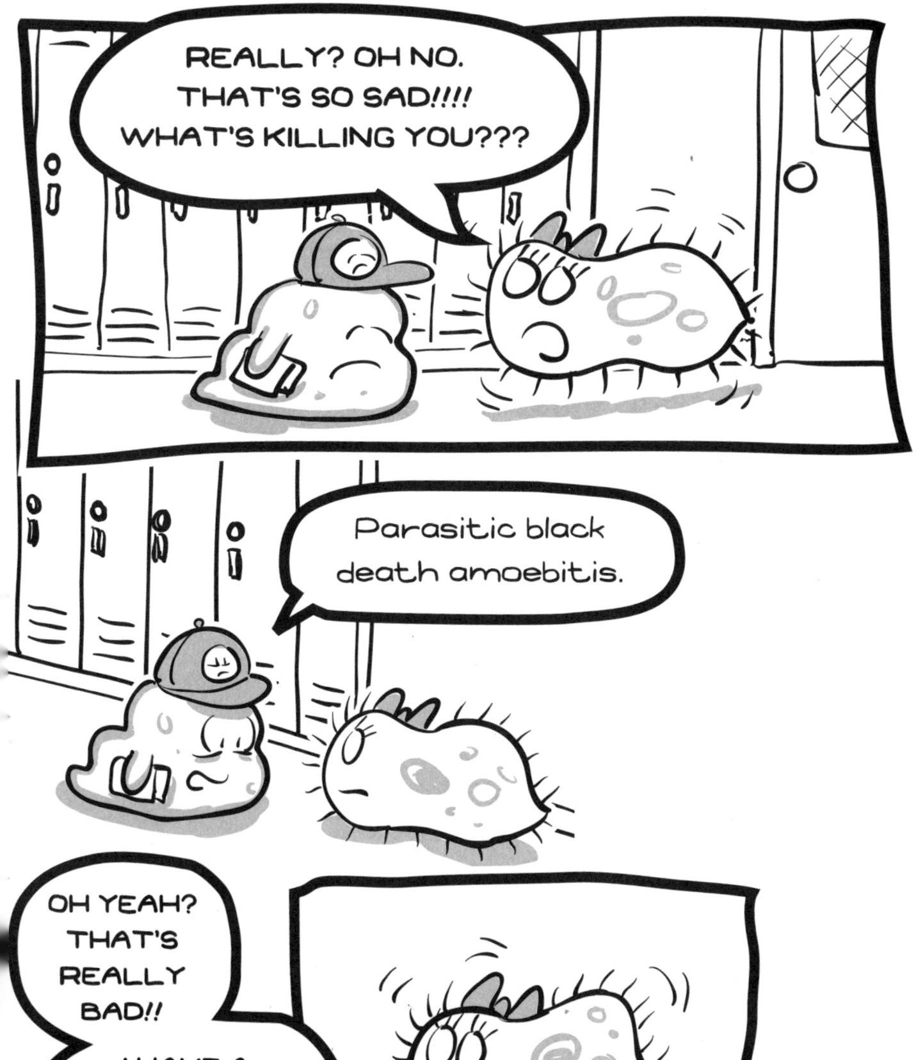
REALLY? OH NO. THAT'S SO SAD!!!! WHAT'S KILLING YOU???
Parasitic black death amoebitis.
OH YEAH? THAT'S REALLY BAD!!
I HAVE A FRIEND WHO HAD A FRIEND WHO DIED FROM THAT!!!!

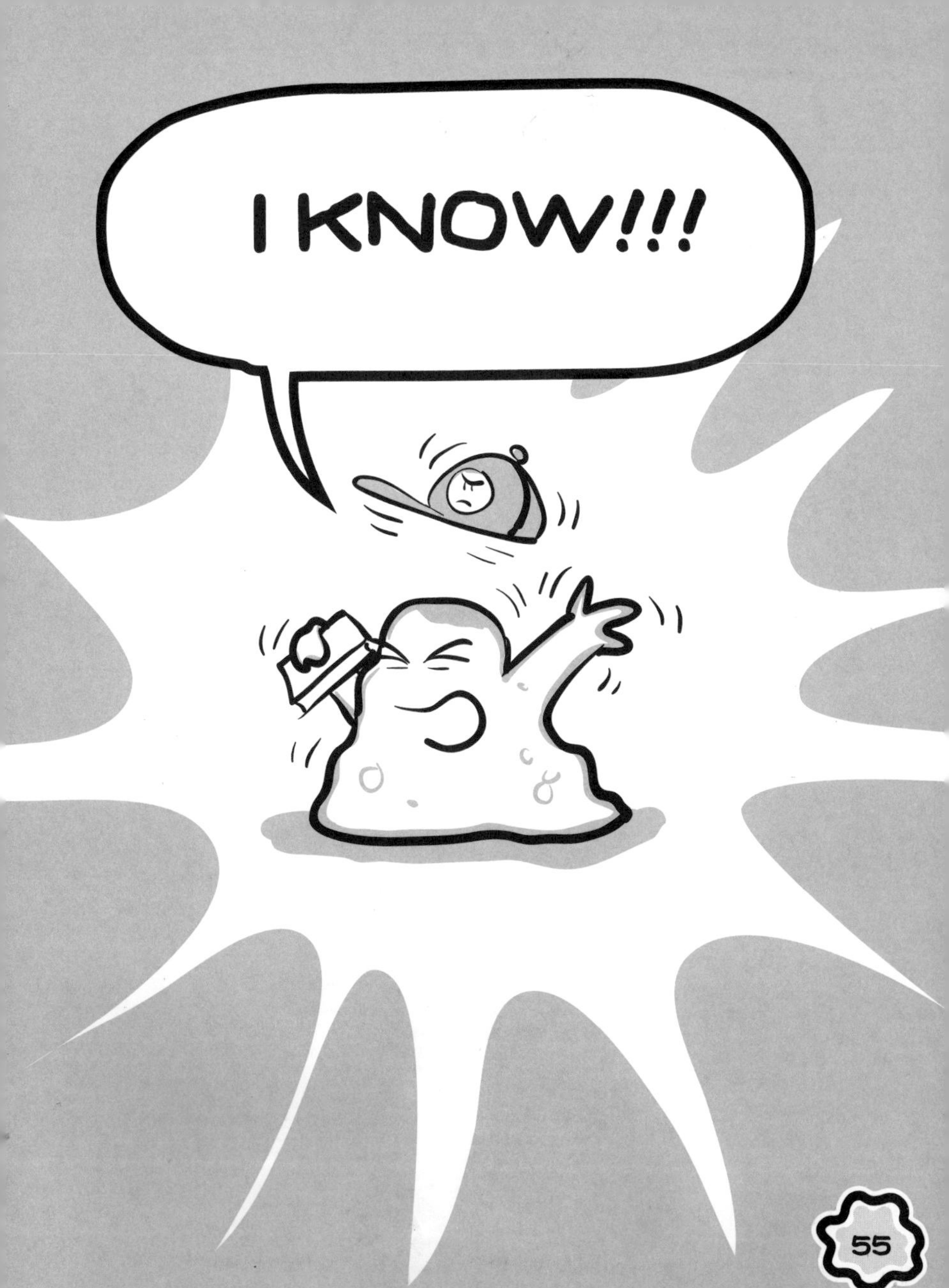
I KNOW!!!

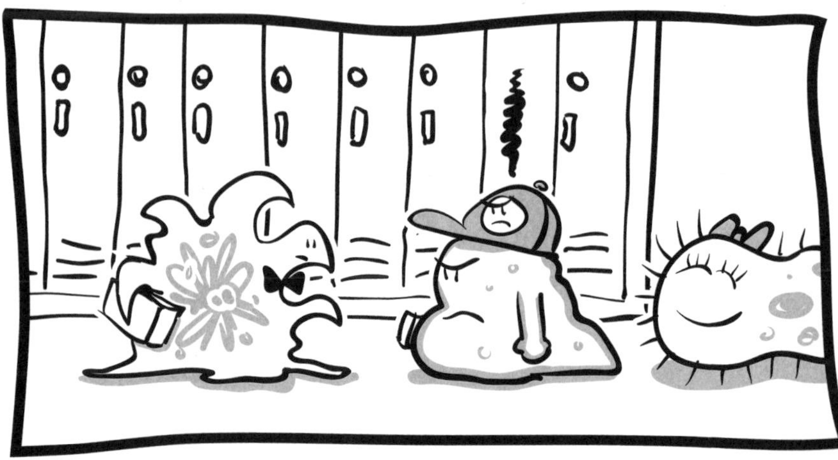

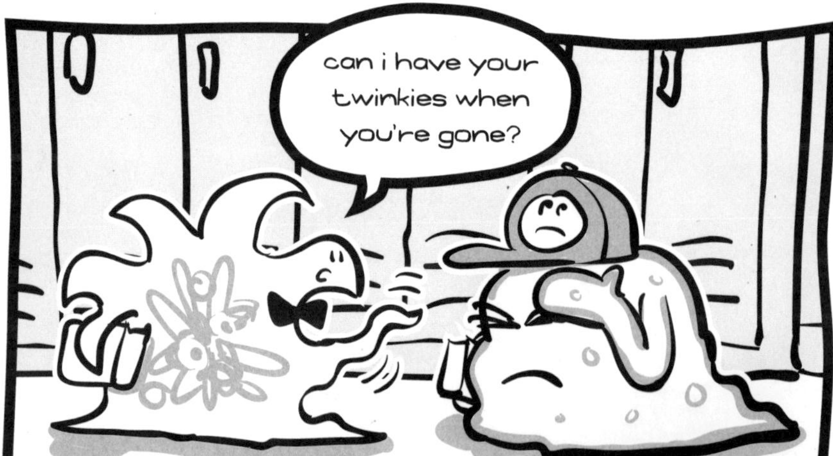
can i have your twinkies when you're gone?

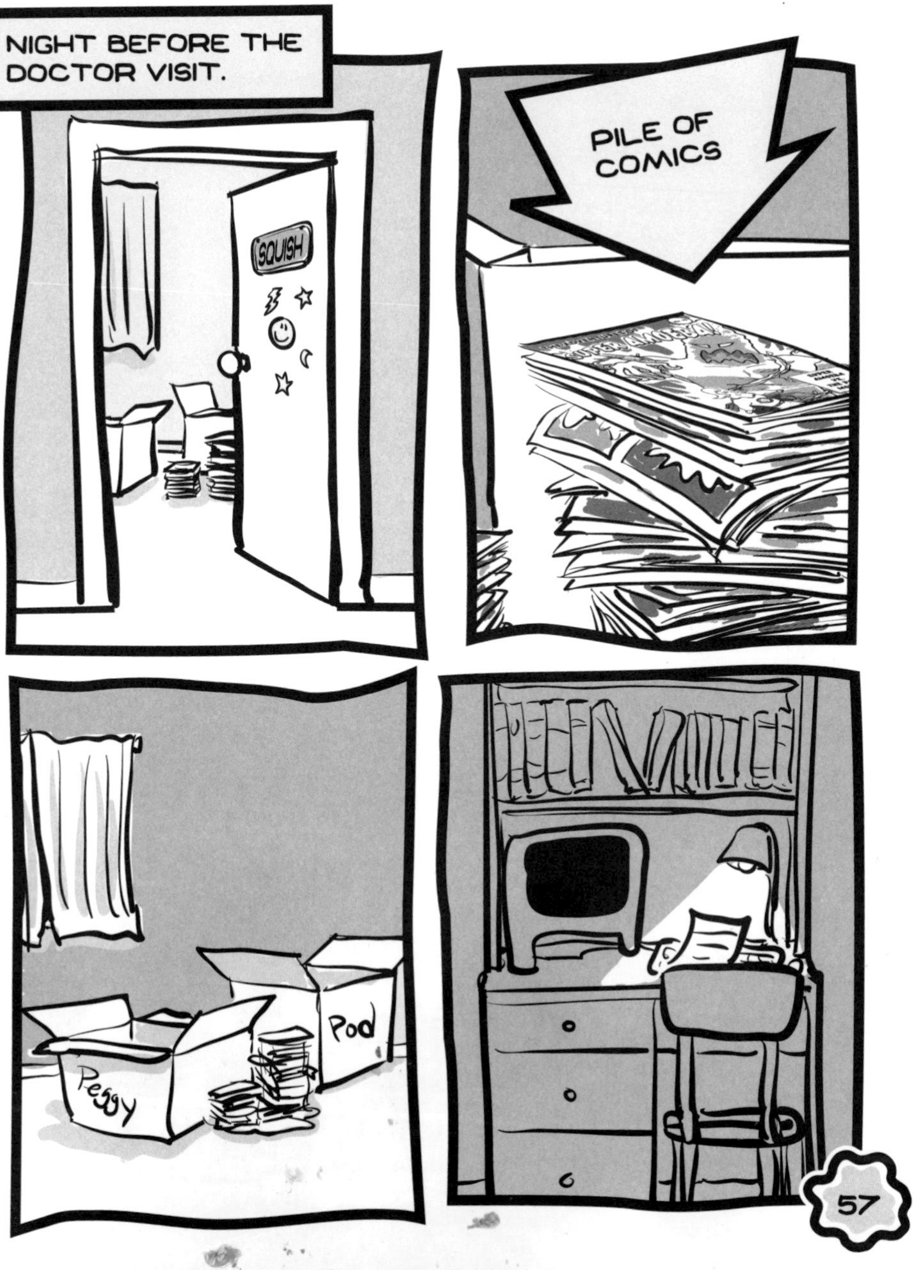
NIGHT BEFORE THE DOCTOR VISIT.
SQUISH
PILE OF COMICS
Peggy
Pod

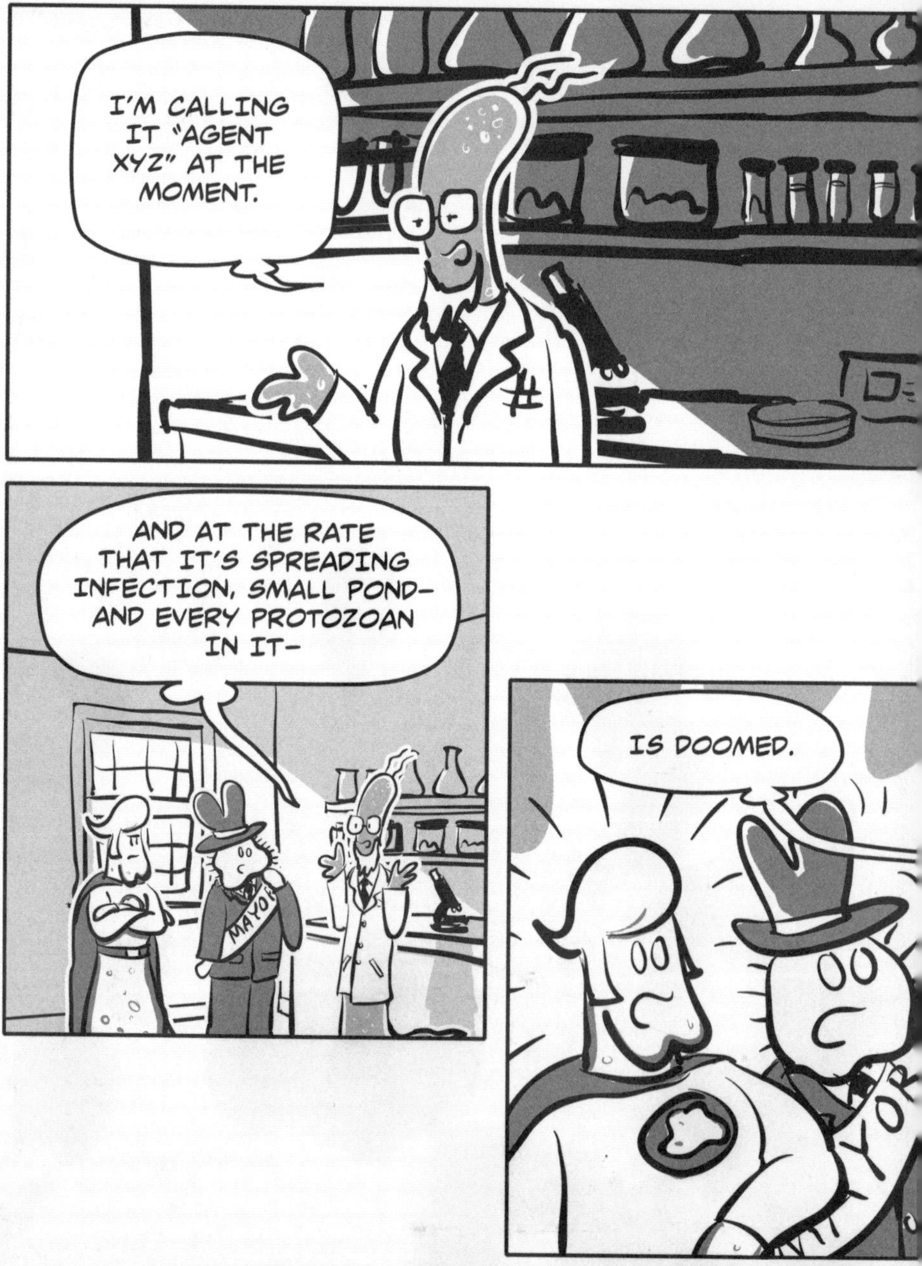
I'M CALLING IT "AGENT XYZ" AT THE MOMENT.
AND AT THE RATE THAT IT'S SPREADING INFECTION, SMALL POND-AND EVERY PROTOZOAN IN IT-
IS DOOMED.

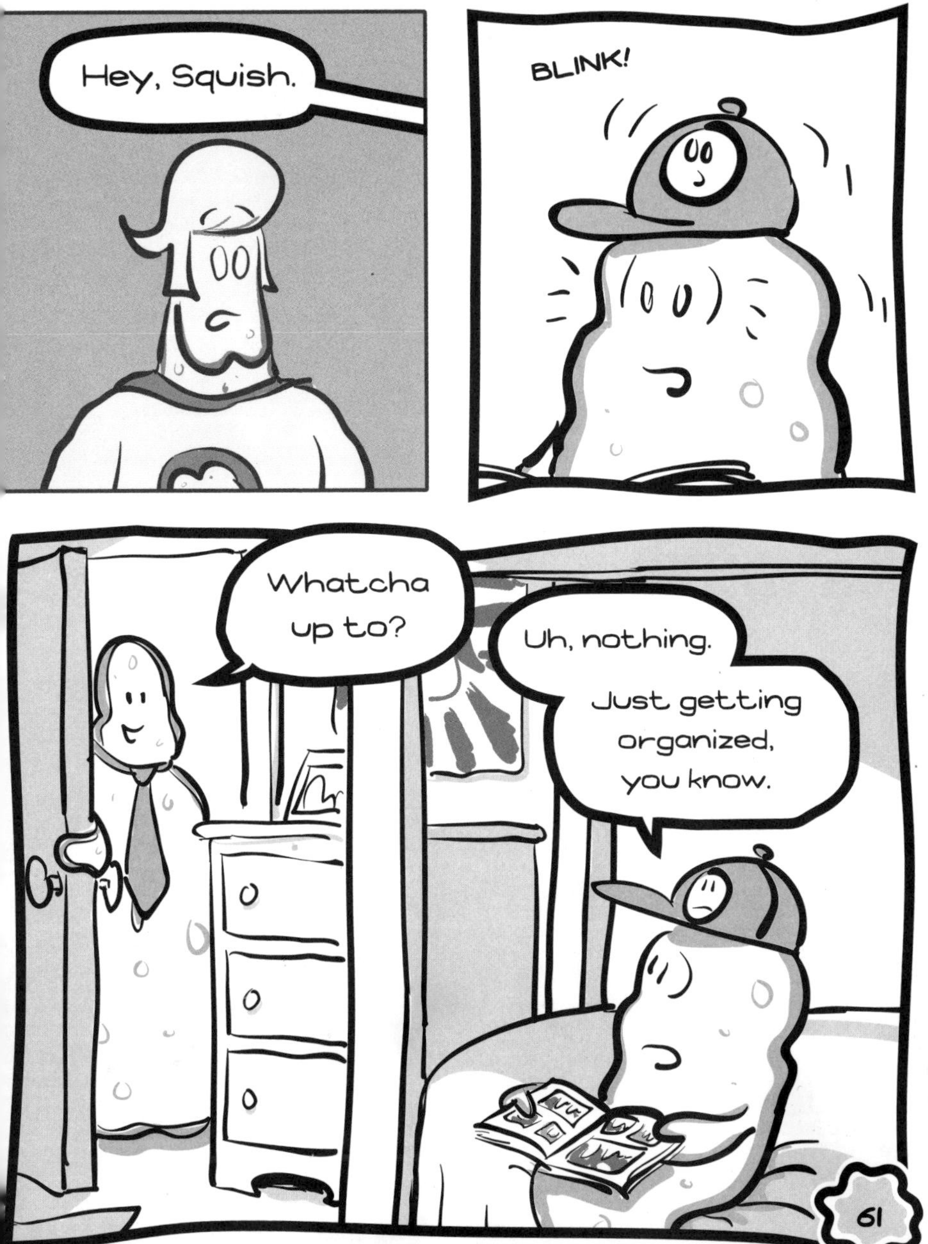
Hey, Squish.
BLINK!
Whatcha up to?
Uh, nothing.
Just getting organized, you know.

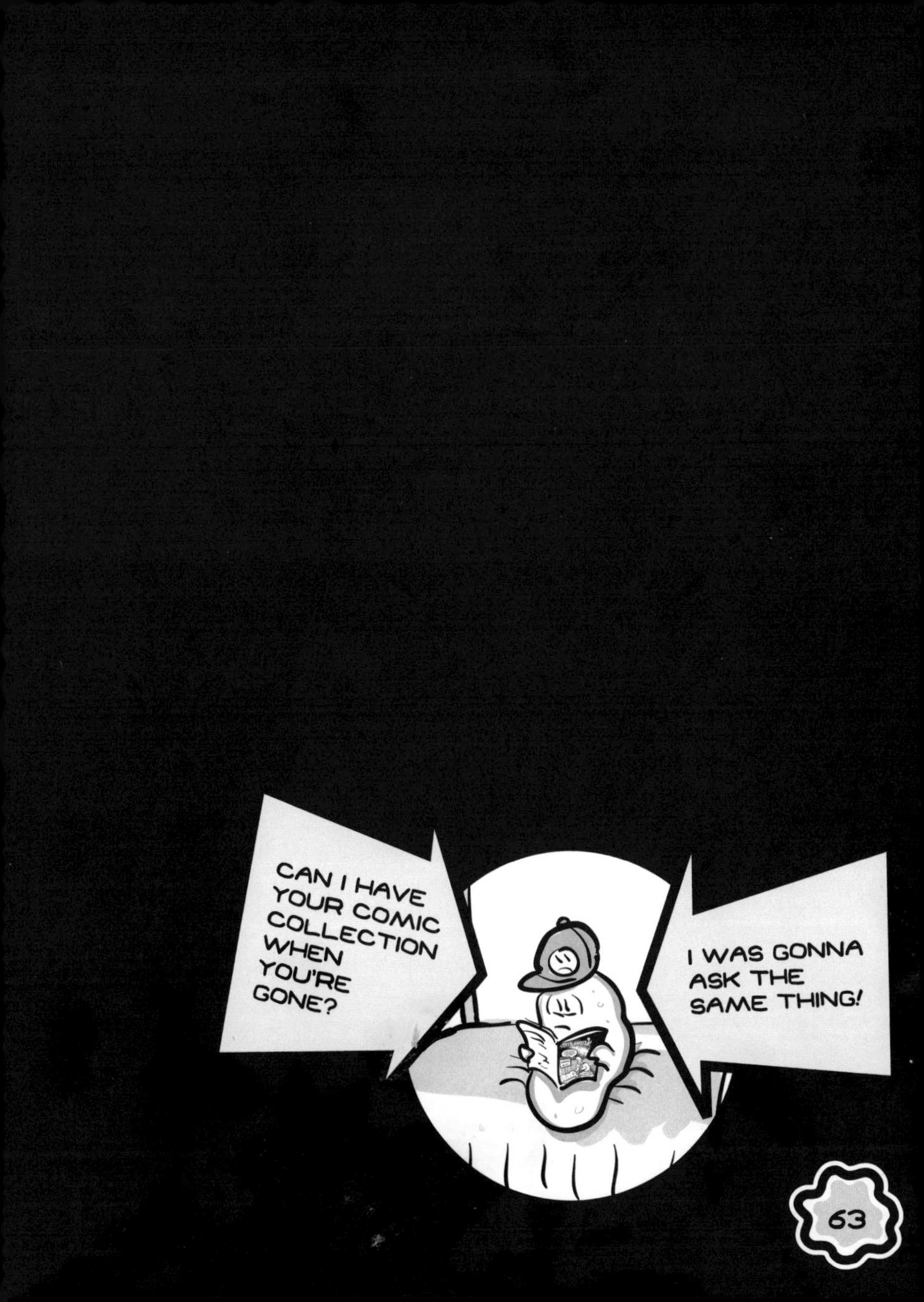
CAN I HAVE YOUR COMIC COLLECTION WHEN YOU'RE GONE?
I WAS GONNA ASK THE SAME THING!

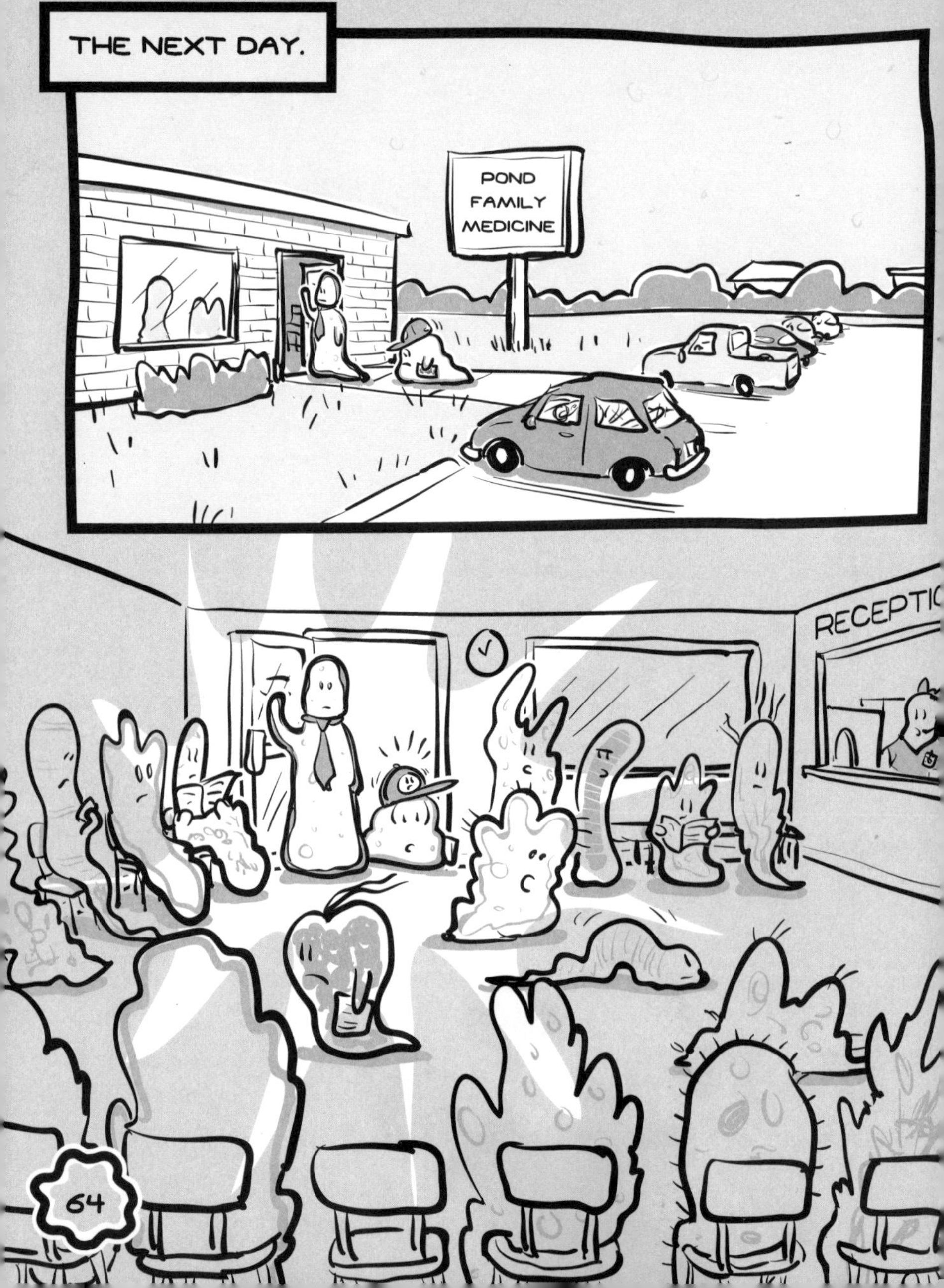
THE NEXT DAY.
POND FAMILY MEDICINE

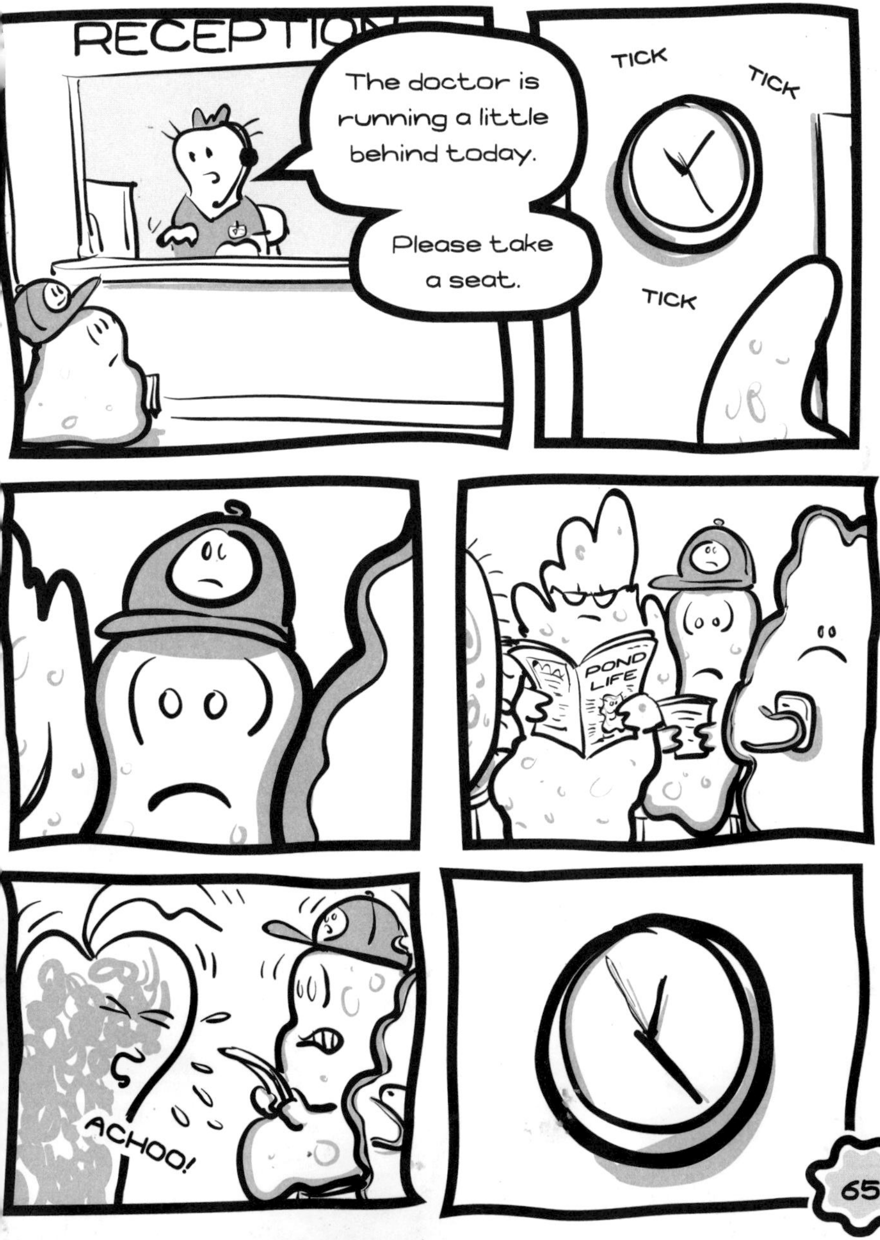
RECEPTION
The doctor is running a little behind today.
Please take a seat.
TICK
TICK
TICK
POND LIFE
ACHOO!

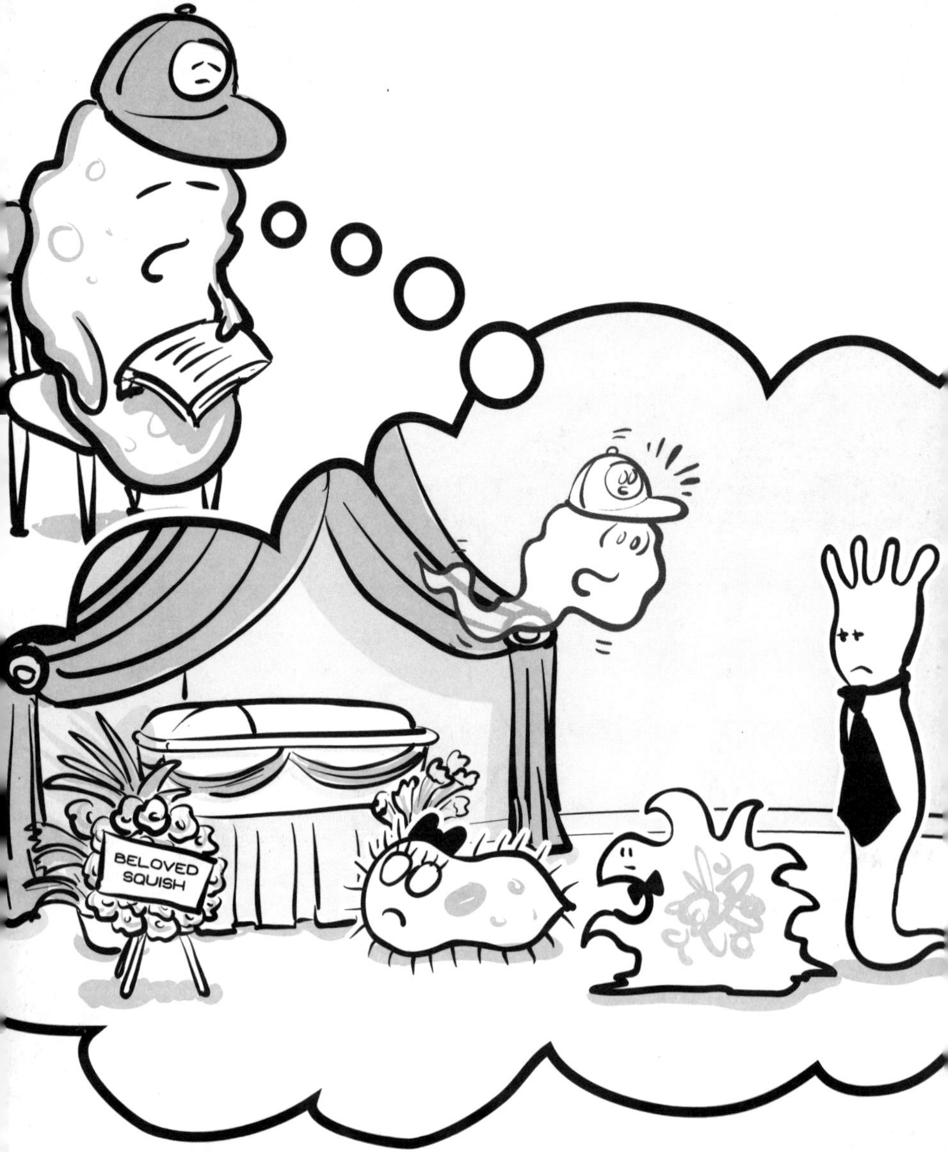
BELOVED SQUISH

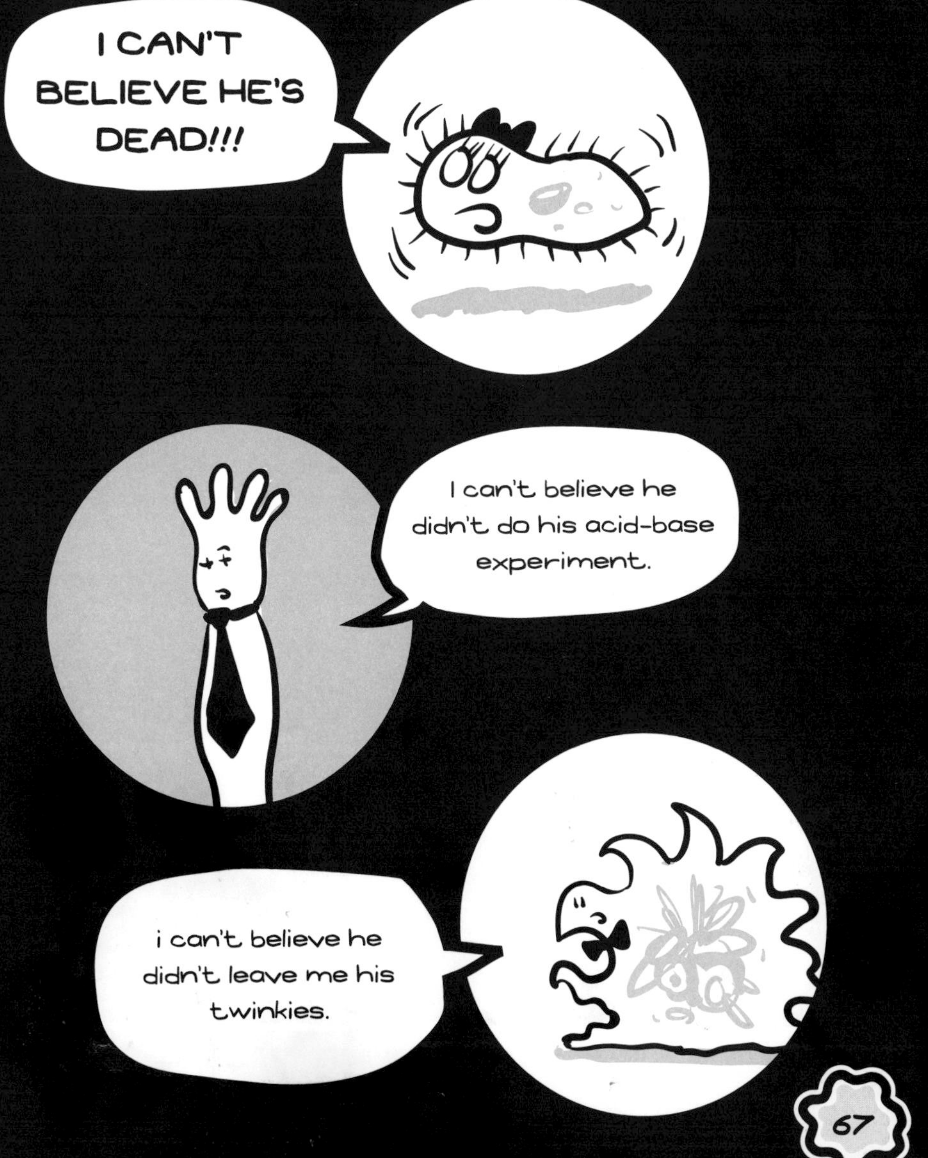

I CAN'T BELIEVE HE'S DEAD!!!
I can't believe he didn't do his acid-base experiment.
i can't believe he didn't leave me his twinkies.

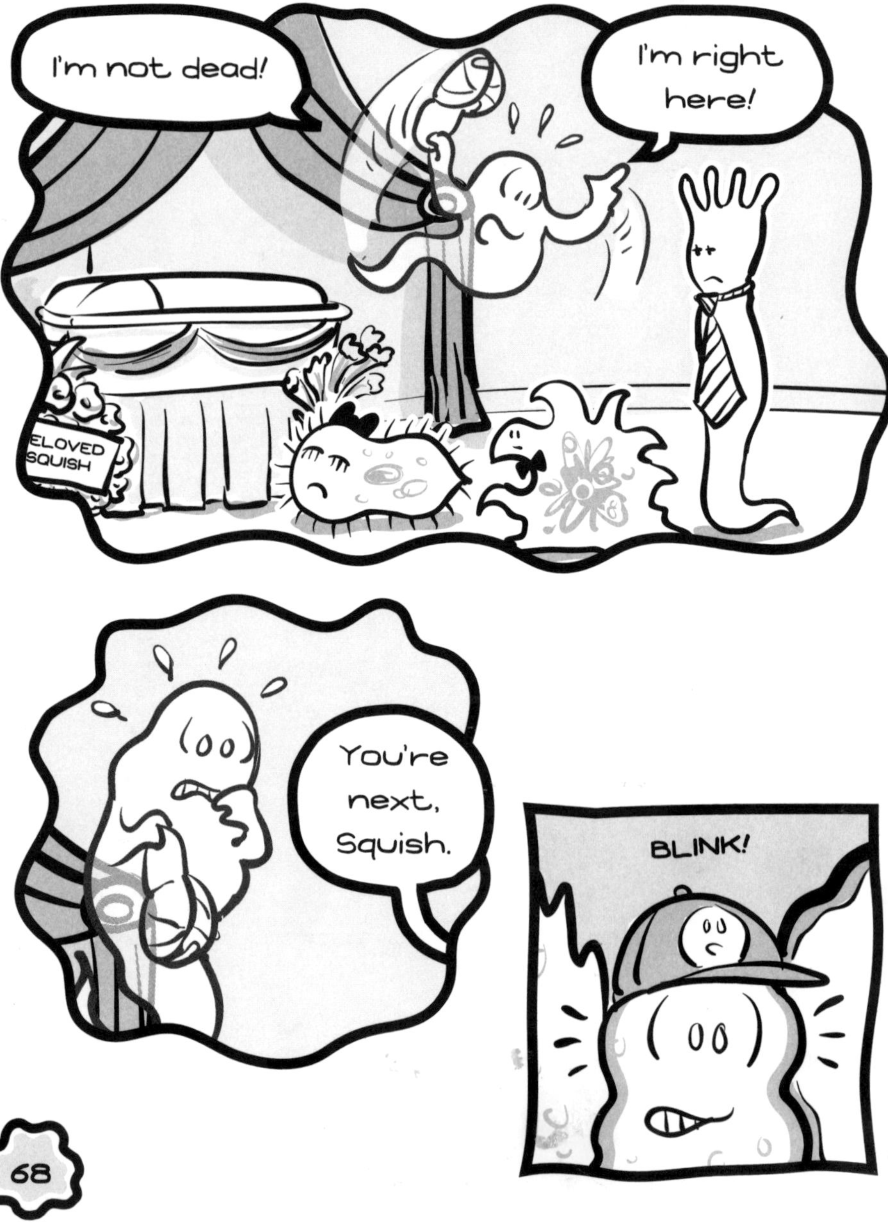
I'm not dead!
I'm right here!
BELOVED SQUISH
You're next, Squish.
BLINK!

69

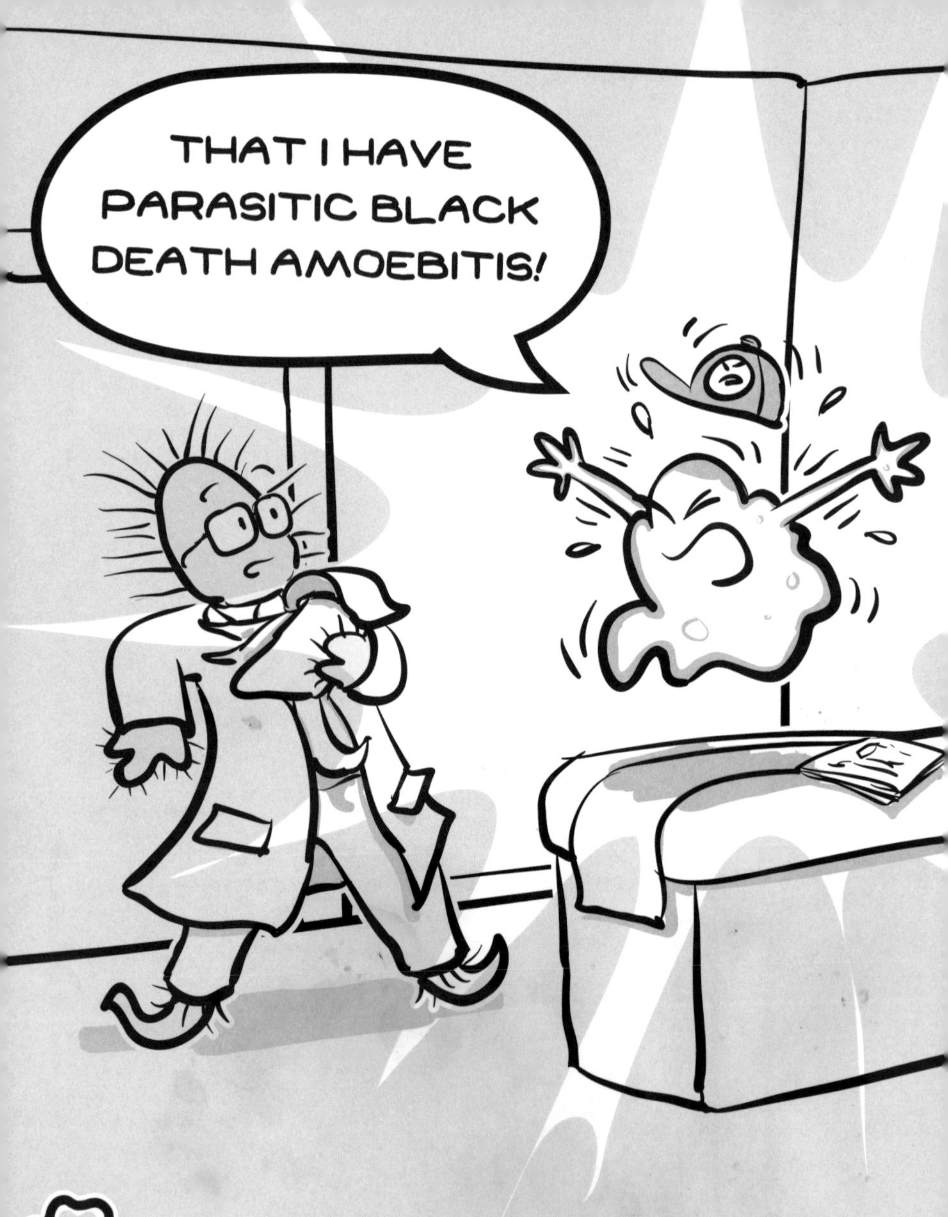
THAT I HAVE PARASITIC BLACK DEATH AMOEBITIS!

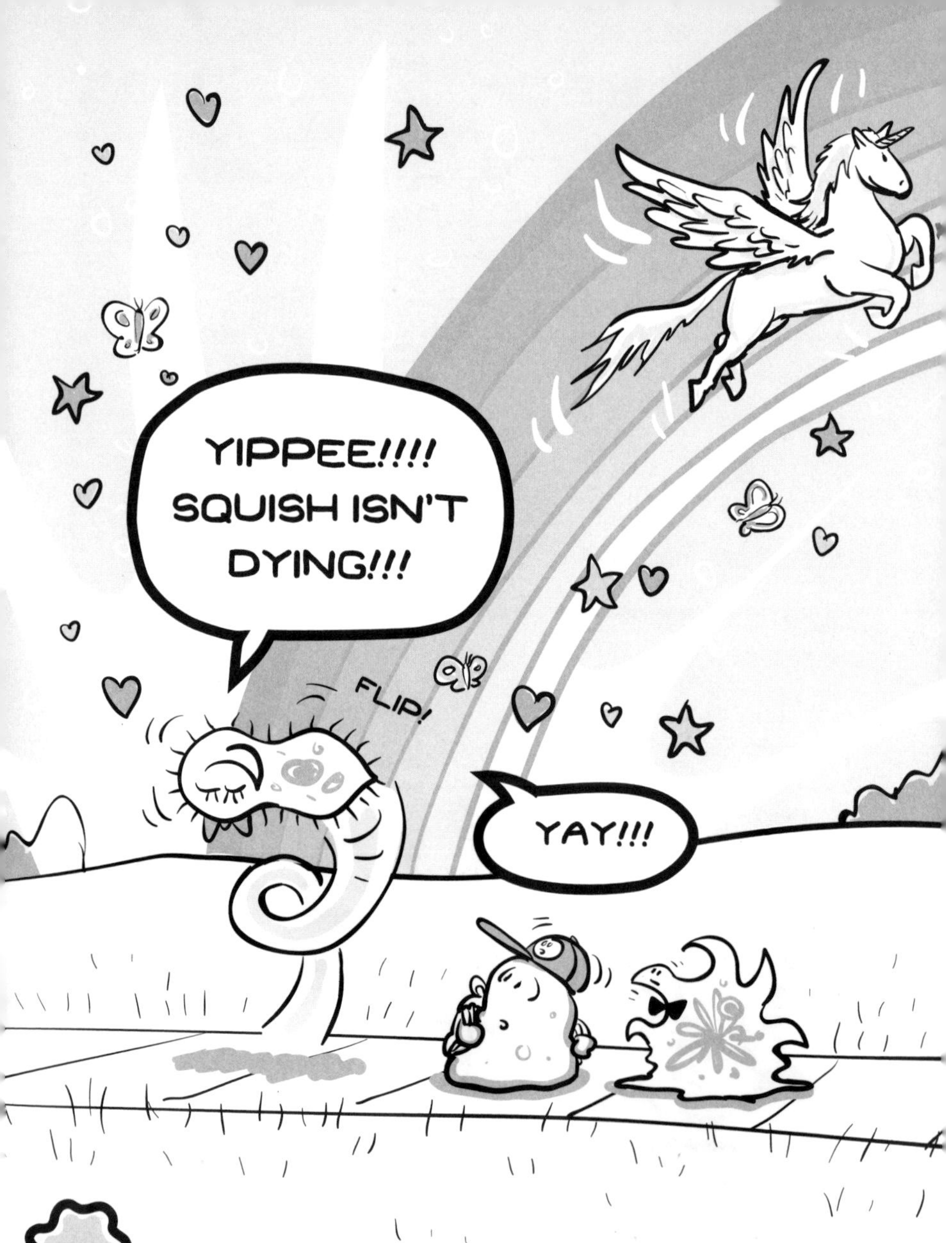
YIPPEE!!!! SQUISH ISN'T DYING!!!
FLIP!
YAY!!!

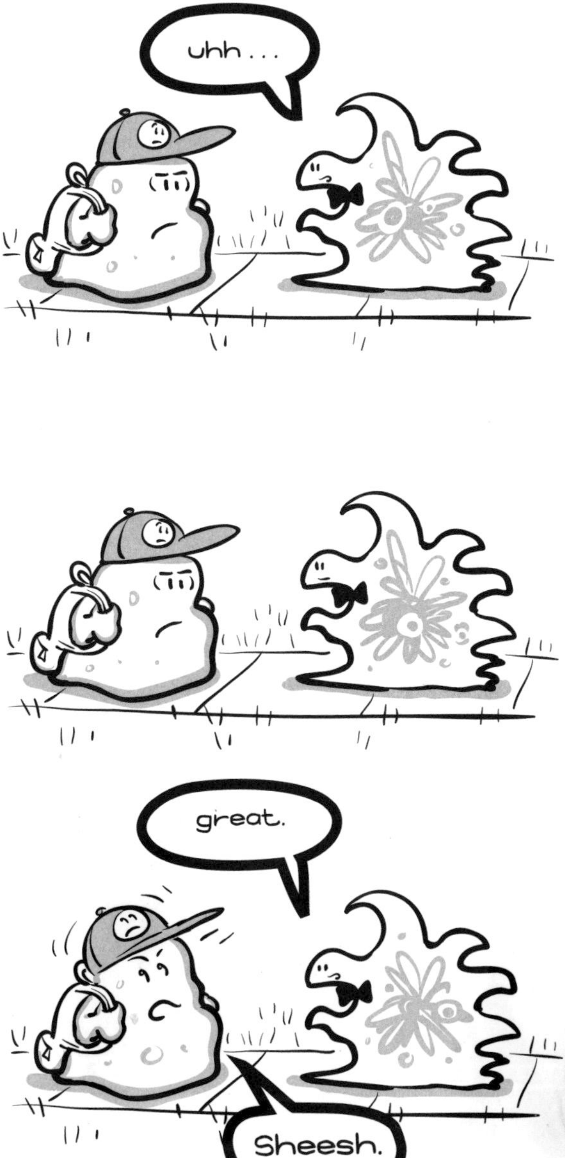
uhh . . .
great.
Sheesh.

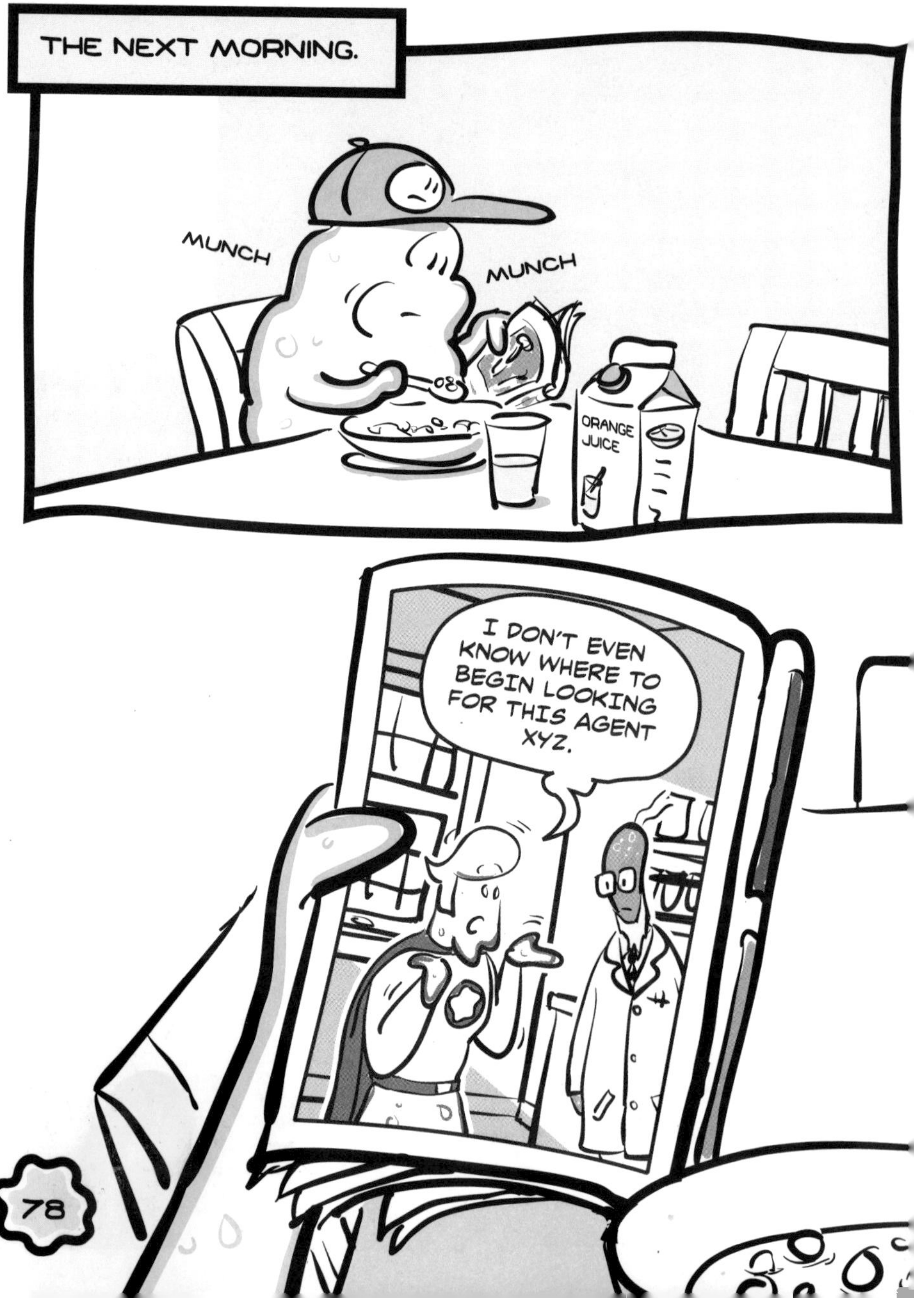
THE NEXT MORNING.
MUNCH
MUNCH
ORANGE JUICE
I DON'T EVEN KNOW WHERE TO BEGIN LOOKING FOR THIS AGENT XYZ.

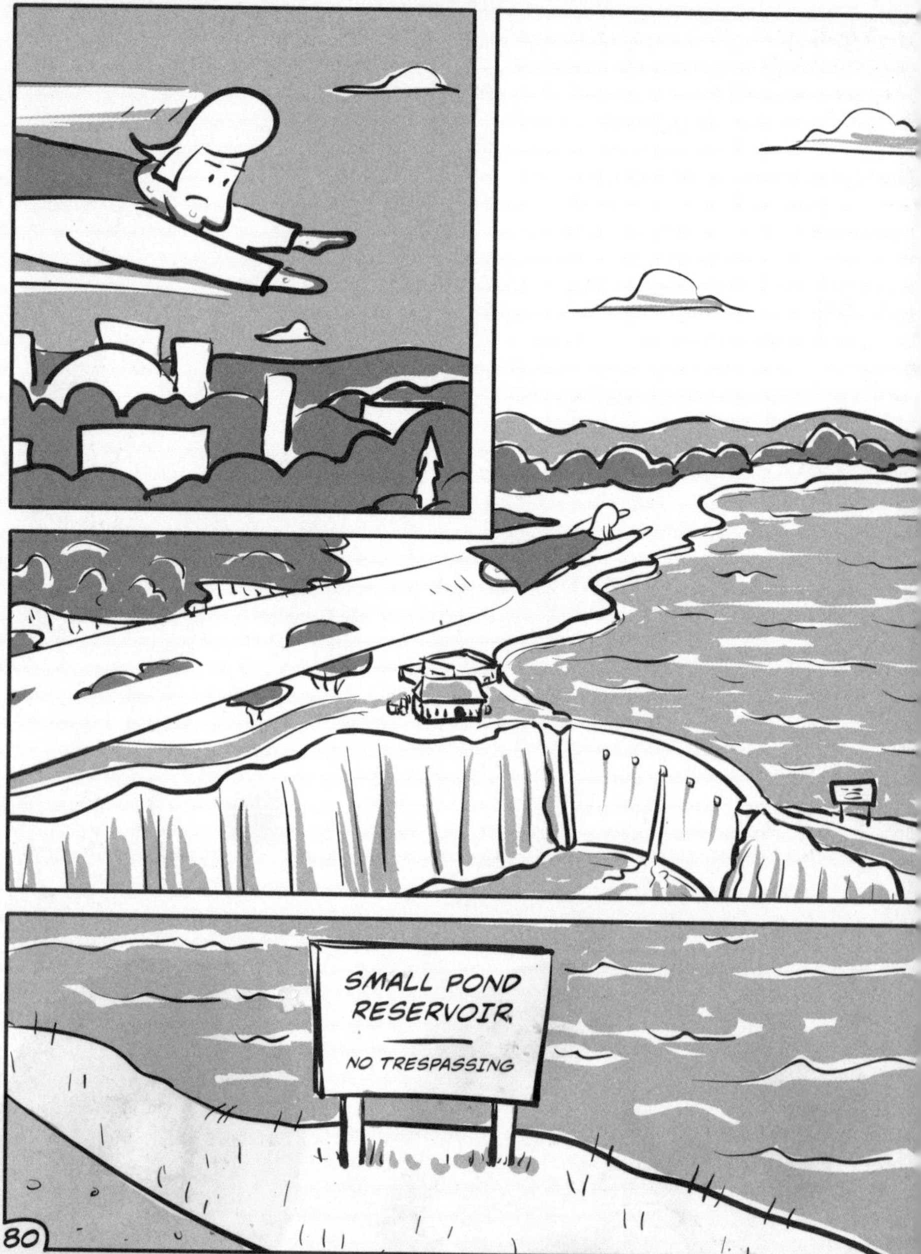
SMALL POND
RESERVOIR
NO TRESPASSING

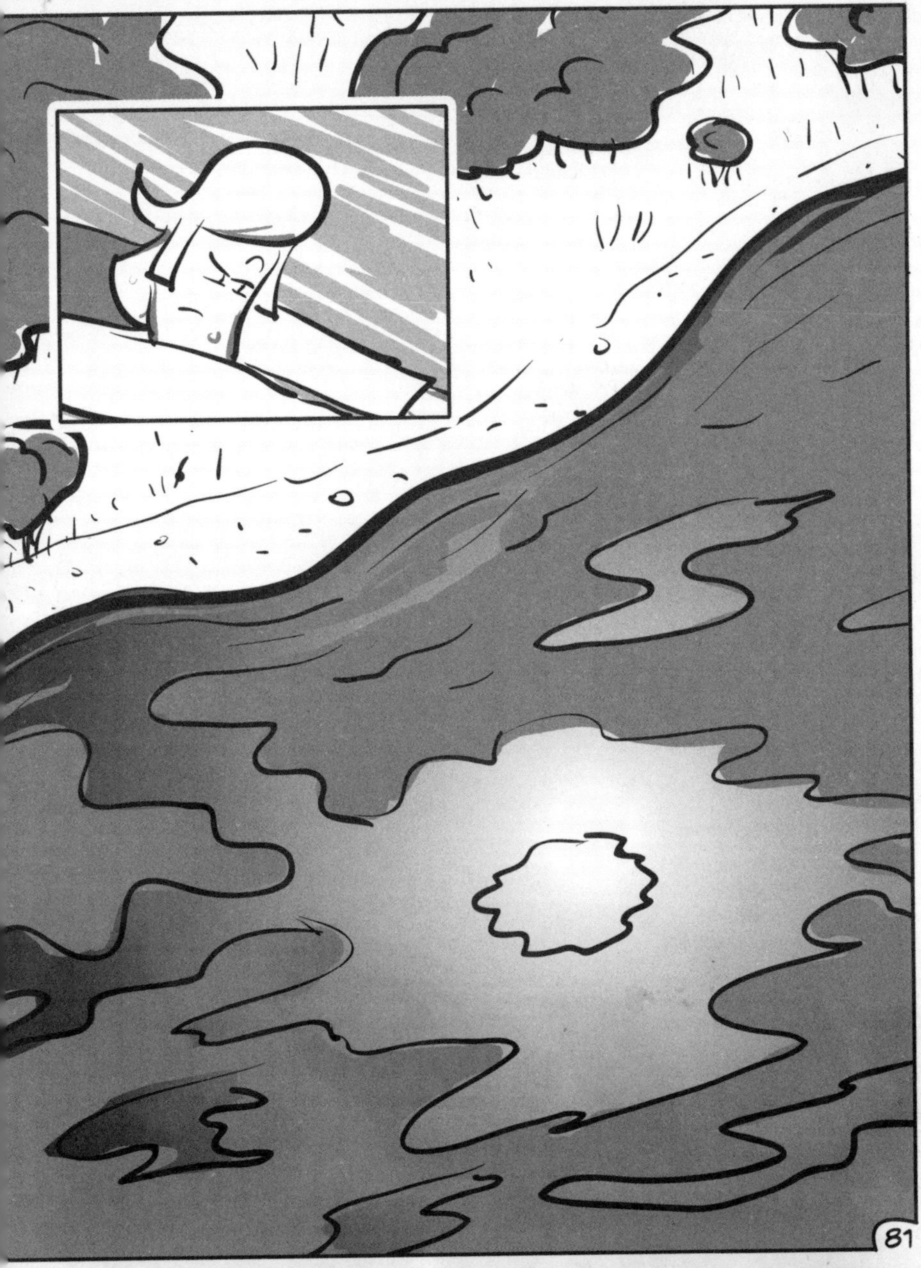

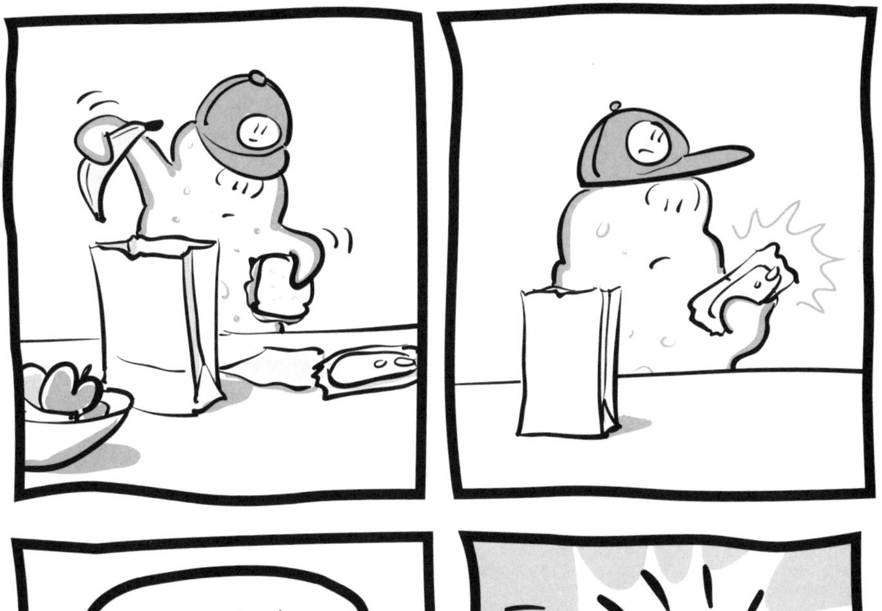
Most obvious place.
RIP!

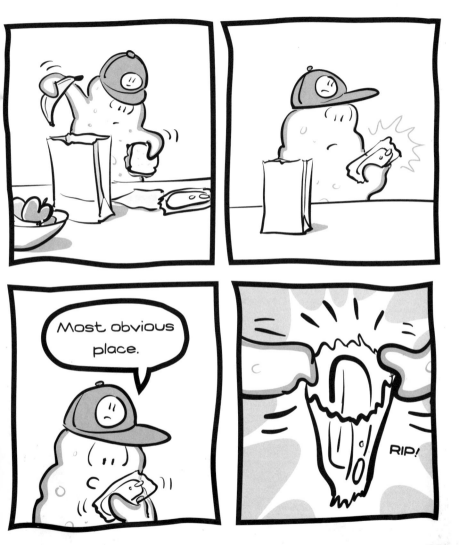

GRAB!

ORANGE JUICE

GULP!

85

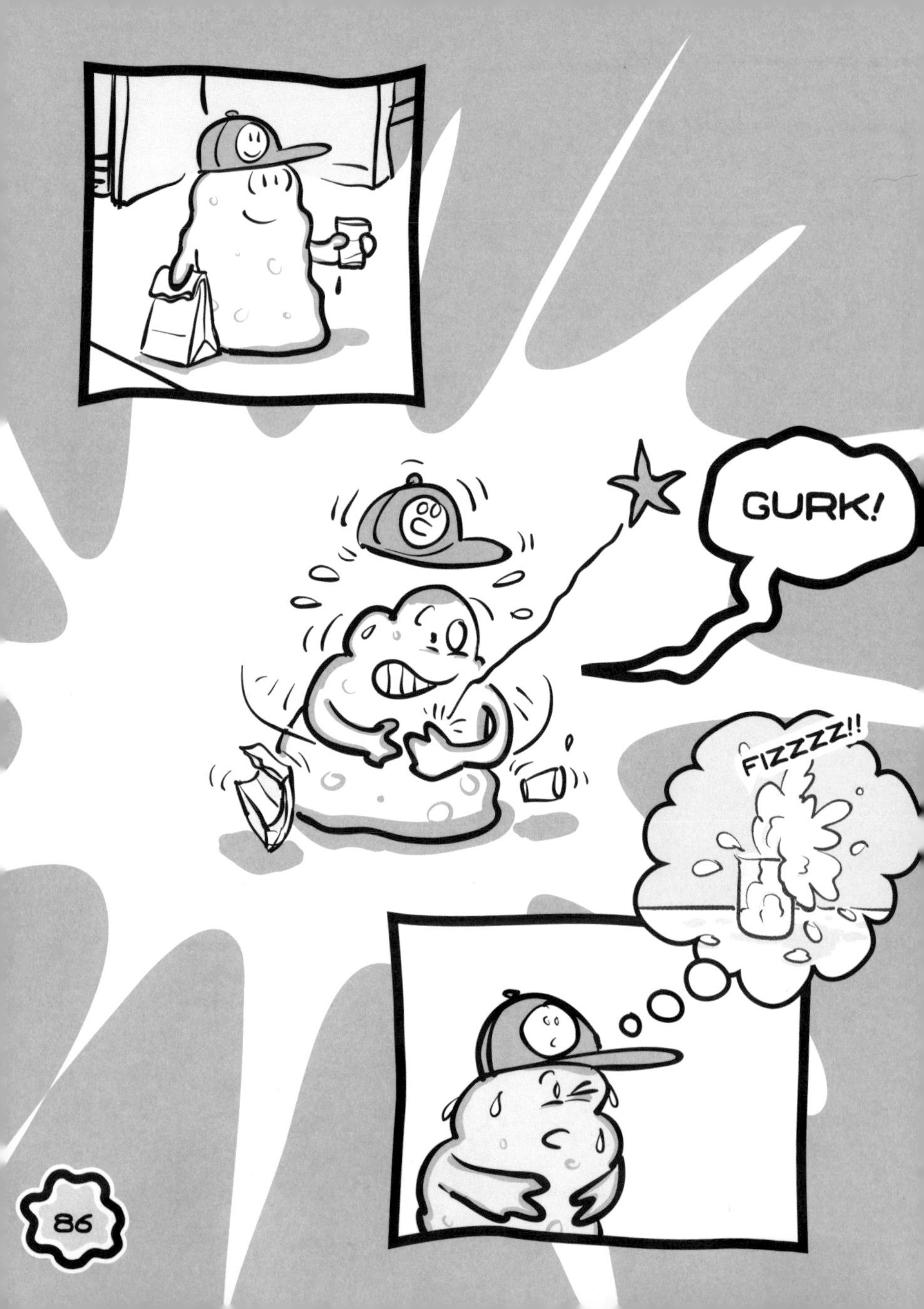
GURK!
FIZZZZ!!

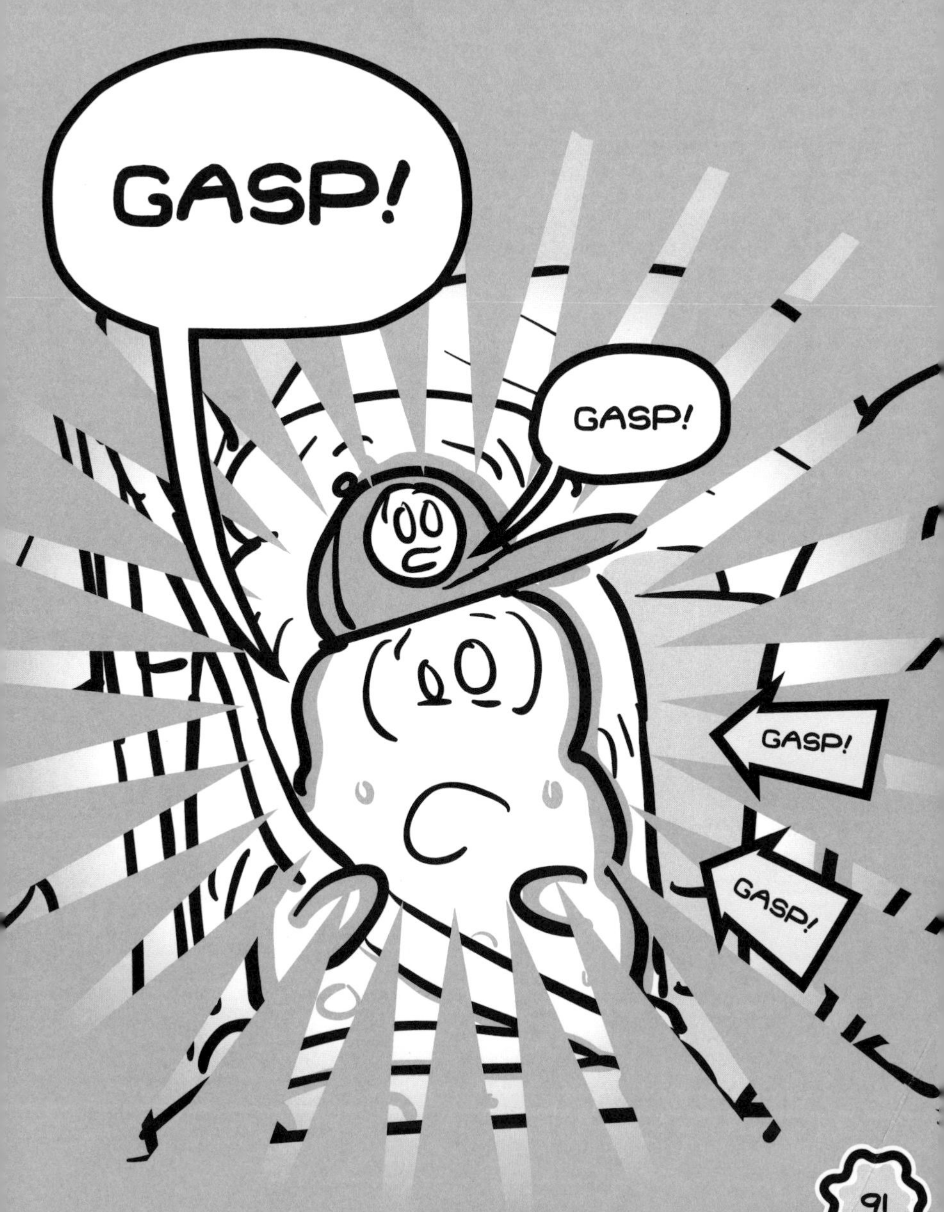
GASP!
GASP!
GASP!
GASP!

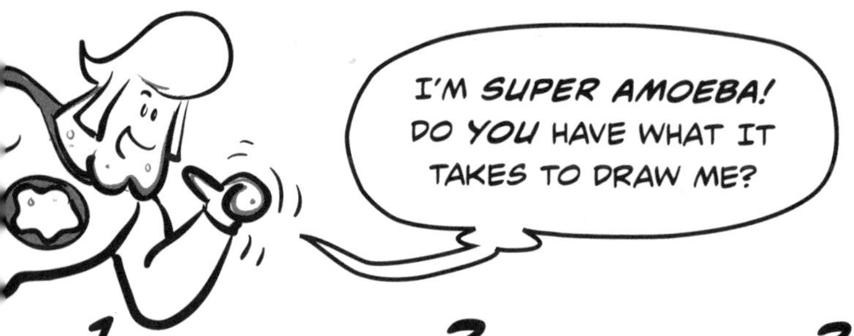
I'M SUPER AMOEBA!
DO YOU HAVE WHAT IT
TAKES TO DRAW ME?

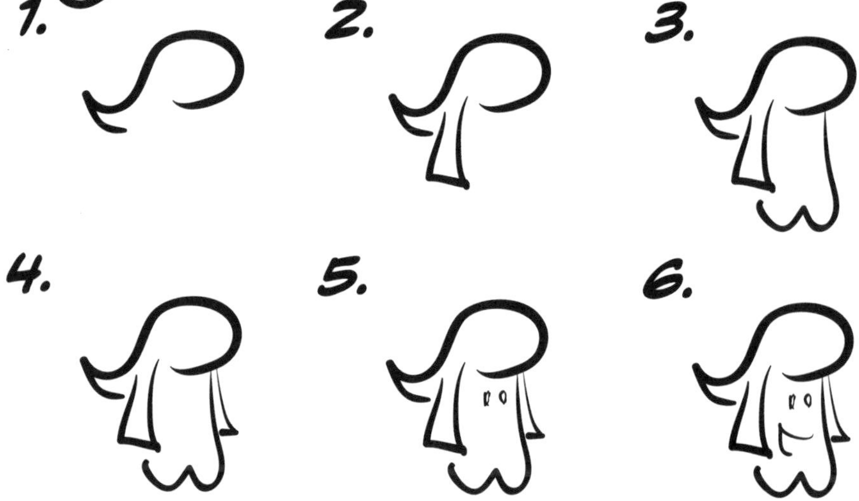
1.
2.
3.
4.
5.
6.

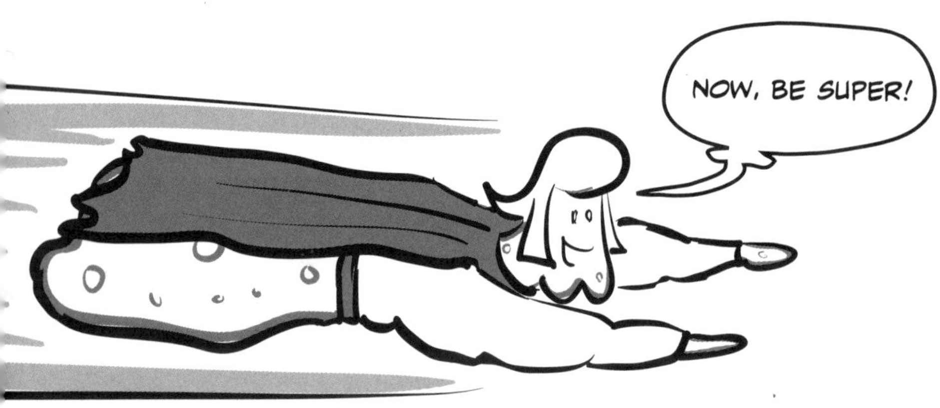
NOW, BE SUPER!

IF YOU LIKE SQUISH, YOU'LL LOVE BABYMOUSE!

#1 BABYMOUSE: Queen of the World!
#2 BABYMOUSE: Our Hero
#3 BABYMOUSE: Beach Babe
#4 BABYMOUSE: Rock Star
#5 BABYMOUSE: Heartbreaker
#6 CAMP BABYMOUSE
#7 BABYMOUSE: Skater Girl
#8 BABYMOUSE: Puppy Love
#9 BABYMOUSE: Monster Mash
#10 BABYMOUSE: The Musical
#11 BABYMOUSE: Dragonslayer
#12 BABYMOUSE: Burns Rubber
#13 BABYMOUSE: Cupcake Tycoon
#14 BABYMOUSE: Mad Scientist
#15 A Very BABYMOUSE Christmas
#16 BABYMOUSE for President
#17 Extreme BABYMOUSE
#18 Happy Birthday, BABYMOUSE
#19 BABYMOUSE: Bad Babysitter

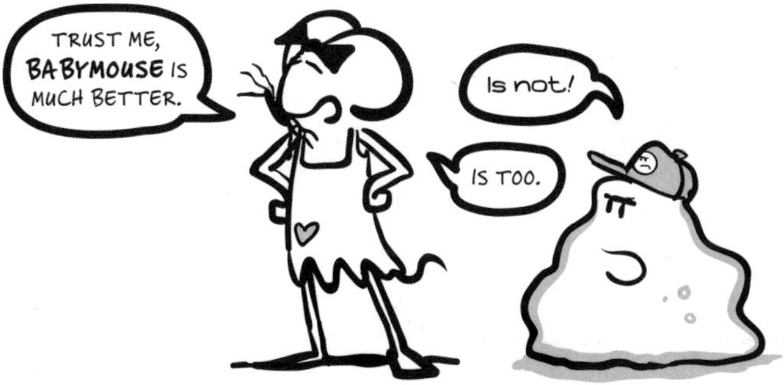
TRUST ME, BABYMOUSE IS MUCH BETTER.
Is not!
IS TOO.